Turk • De Groot

CLIFTON
7 DAYS TO DIE

9th CINEBOOK
The 9th Art Publisher

Original title : 7 jours pour mourir – CLIFTON

Original edition : ©1979 LE LOMBARD (Dargaud – Lombard s.a.) by DE GROOT & TURK
www.lelombard.com

English translation: © 2005 Cinebook Ltd

Translator: Luke Spear
Lettering and Text layout: Info Elec sarl
Printed in Belgium by Proost Fleurus

This edition first published in Great Britain in 2006 by
CINEBOOK Ltd
PO Box 293, 18 John Dutton Way
Ashford, Kent
TN23 9AD
www.cinebook.co.uk

A CIP catalogue record for this book
is available from the British Library

ISBN 1-905460-08-2

9th CINEBOOK
The 9th Art Publisher

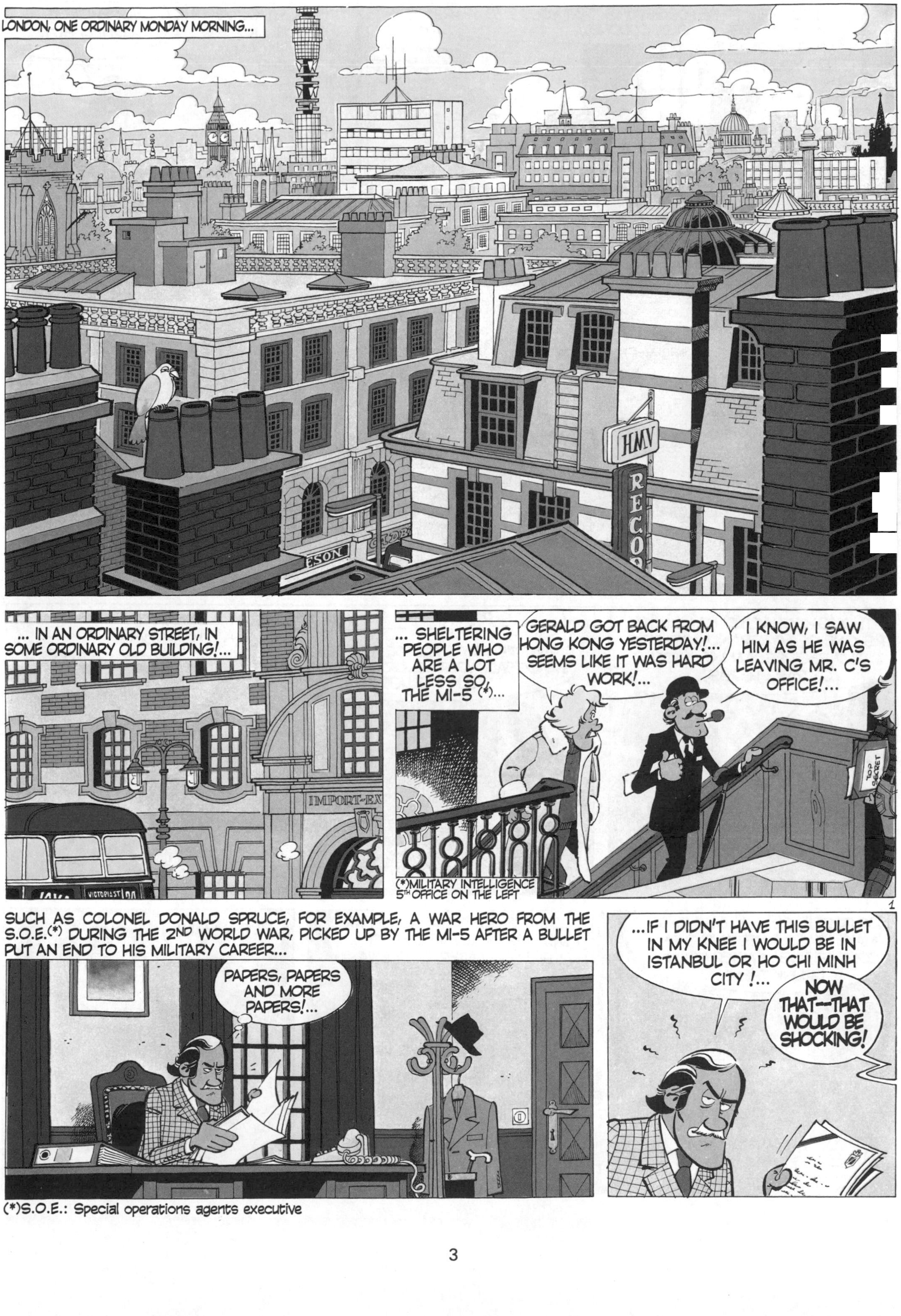
LONDON, ONE ORDINARY MONDAY MORNING...
HMV
... IN AN ORDINARY STREET, IN SOME ORDINARY OLD BUILDING!...
... SHELTERING PEOPLE WHO ARE A LOT LESS SO, THE MI-5 (*)...
GERALD GOT BACK FROM HONG KONG YESTERDAY!... SEEMS LIKE IT WAS HARD WORK!...
I KNOW, I SAW HIM AS HE WAS LEAVING MR. C'S OFFICE!...
TOP SECRET
(*)MILITARY INTELLIGENCE 5TH OFFICE ON THE LEFT
SUCH AS COLONEL DONALD SPRUCE, FOR EXAMPLE, A WAR HERO FROM THE S.O.E.(*) DURING THE 2ND WORLD WAR, PICKED UP BY THE MI-5 AFTER A BULLET PUT AN END TO HIS MILITARY CAREER...
PAPERS, PAPERS AND MORE PAPERS!...
...IF I DIDN'T HAVE THIS BULLET IN MY KNEE I WOULD BE IN ISTANBUL OR HO CHI MINH CITY !...
NOW THAT--THAT WOULD BE SHOCKING!

(*)S.O.E.: Special operations agents executive

YOU SEEM TO BE FORGETTING THAT YOU'RE 53 YEARS OLD, COLONEL!...
MISS MOONISH!... DO YOU MIND!...
JUST COME OUT AND SAY IT, I'M AN OLDIE!
FAR FROM IT, COLONEL, BUT...
?
PFRRT
YOU CALL THAT TEA, DO YOU?
NO!
SO, FOR ONCE WE AGREE!
I THOUGHT THAT YOU'D LIKE IT! IT'S ONE OF MY GRANDMOTHER'S OLD RECIPES: AN INFUSION OF RARE HERBS!...
PAPERWORK, HERBAL TEA! GREAT!... WHAT NEXT? A WHEELCHAIR?
BUT IT'S VERY GOOD FOR YOUR HEALTH, IT BRINGS BACK YOUR MEMORY AND INVIGORATES YOUR INTELLIGENCE!...
NOT POSSIBLE!?... IN THAT CASE, MAKE UP 50 PINTS AND THEN COME SEE ME!... AFTER YOU'VE DRUNK THEM!...
COL. SPRUCE
...AND IF SOMEONE ASKS FOR ME, I AM IN ACTIVE SERVICE!... SEE YOU LATER, LUCREZIA BORGIA!...
COL. SPRUCE
FILTHY MAN!
SLAM

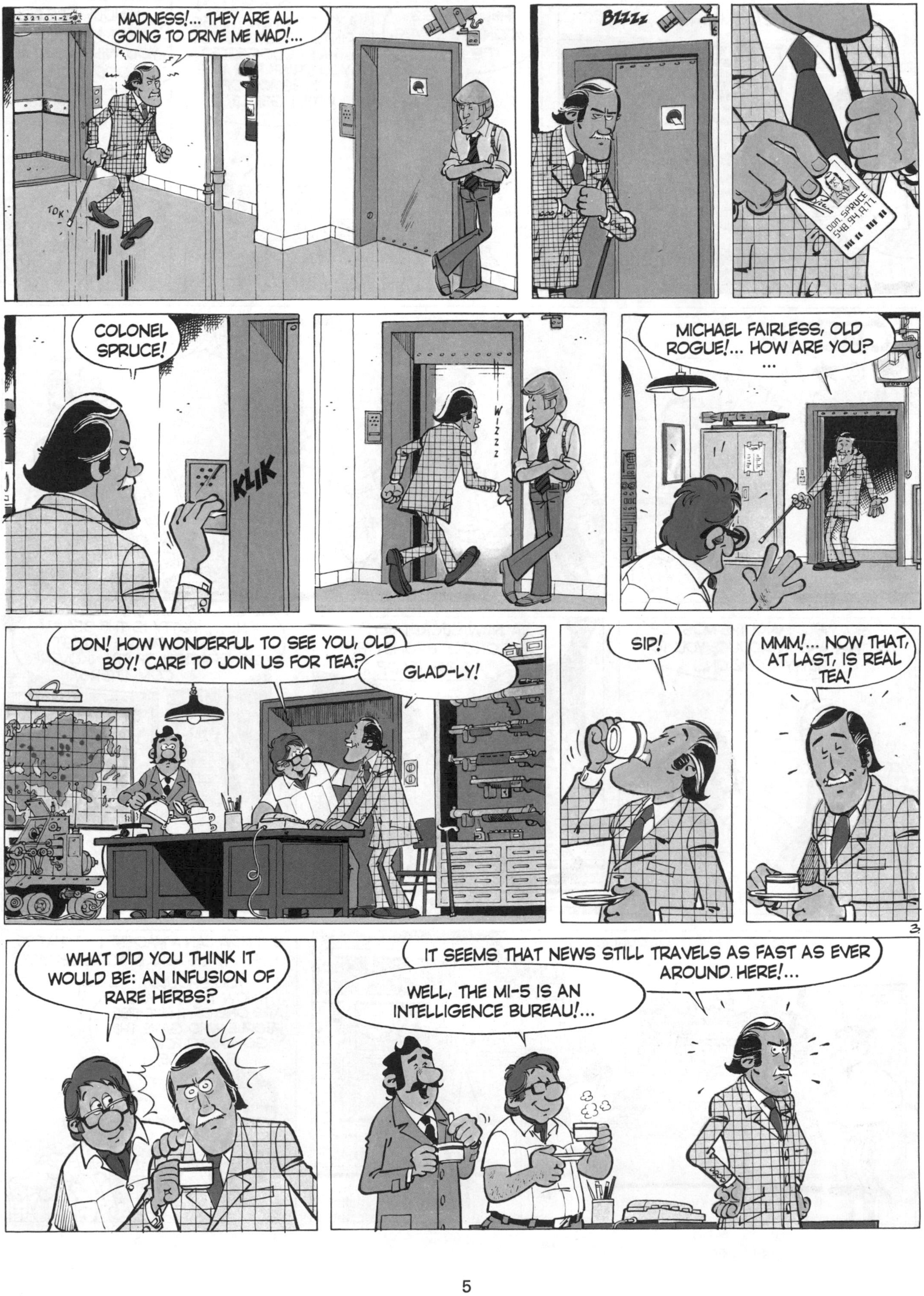
MADNESS!... THEY ARE ALL GOING TO DRIVE ME MAD!...
TOK
BZZZZ
DON. SPRUCE 548.94.A.77
COLONEL SPRUCE!
KLIK
WIZZZ
MICHAEL FAIRLESS, OLD ROGUE!... HOW ARE YOU? ...
DON! HOW WONDERFUL TO SEE YOU, OLD BOY! CARE TO JOIN US FOR TEA?
GLAD-LY!
SIP!
MMM!... NOW THAT, AT LAST, IS REAL TEA!
WHAT DID YOU THINK IT WOULD BE: AN INFUSION OF RARE HERBS?
IT SEEMS THAT NEWS STILL TRAVELS AS FAST AS EVER AROUND HERE!...
WELL, THE MI-5 IS AN INTELLIGENCE BUREAU!...

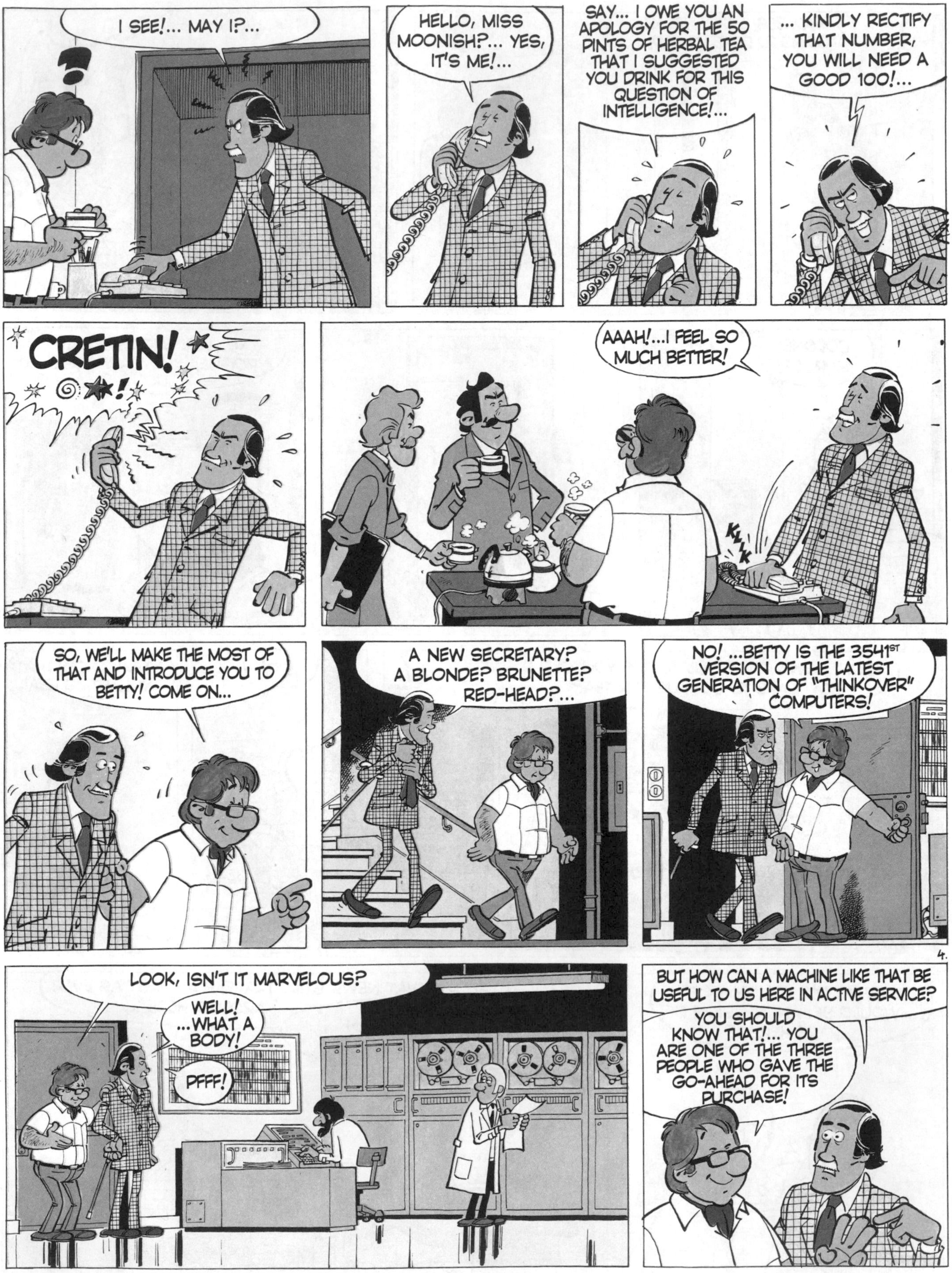
I SEE!... MAY I?...
HELLO, MISS MOONISH?... YES, IT'S ME!...
SAY... I OWE YOU AN APOLOGY FOR THE 50 PINTS OF HERBAL TEA THAT I SUGGESTED YOU DRINK FOR THIS QUESTION OF INTELLIGENCE!...
... KINDLY RECTIFY THAT NUMBER, YOU WILL NEED A GOOD 100!...
CRETIN!
AAAH!...I FEEL SO MUCH BETTER!
KLIK
SO, WE'LL MAKE THE MOST OF THAT AND INTRODUCE YOU TO BETTY! COME ON...
A NEW SECRETARY? A BLONDE? BRUNETTE? RED-HEAD?...
NO! ...BETTY IS THE 3541ST VERSION OF THE LATEST GENERATION OF "THINKOVER" COMPUTERS!
LOOK, ISN'T IT MARVELOUS?
WELL! ...WHAT A BODY!
PFFF!
BUT HOW CAN A MACHINE LIKE THAT BE USEFUL TO US HERE IN ACTIVE SERVICE?
YOU SHOULD KNOW THAT!... YOU ARE ONE OF THE THREE PEOPLE WHO GAVE THE GO-AHEAD FOR ITS PURCHASE!

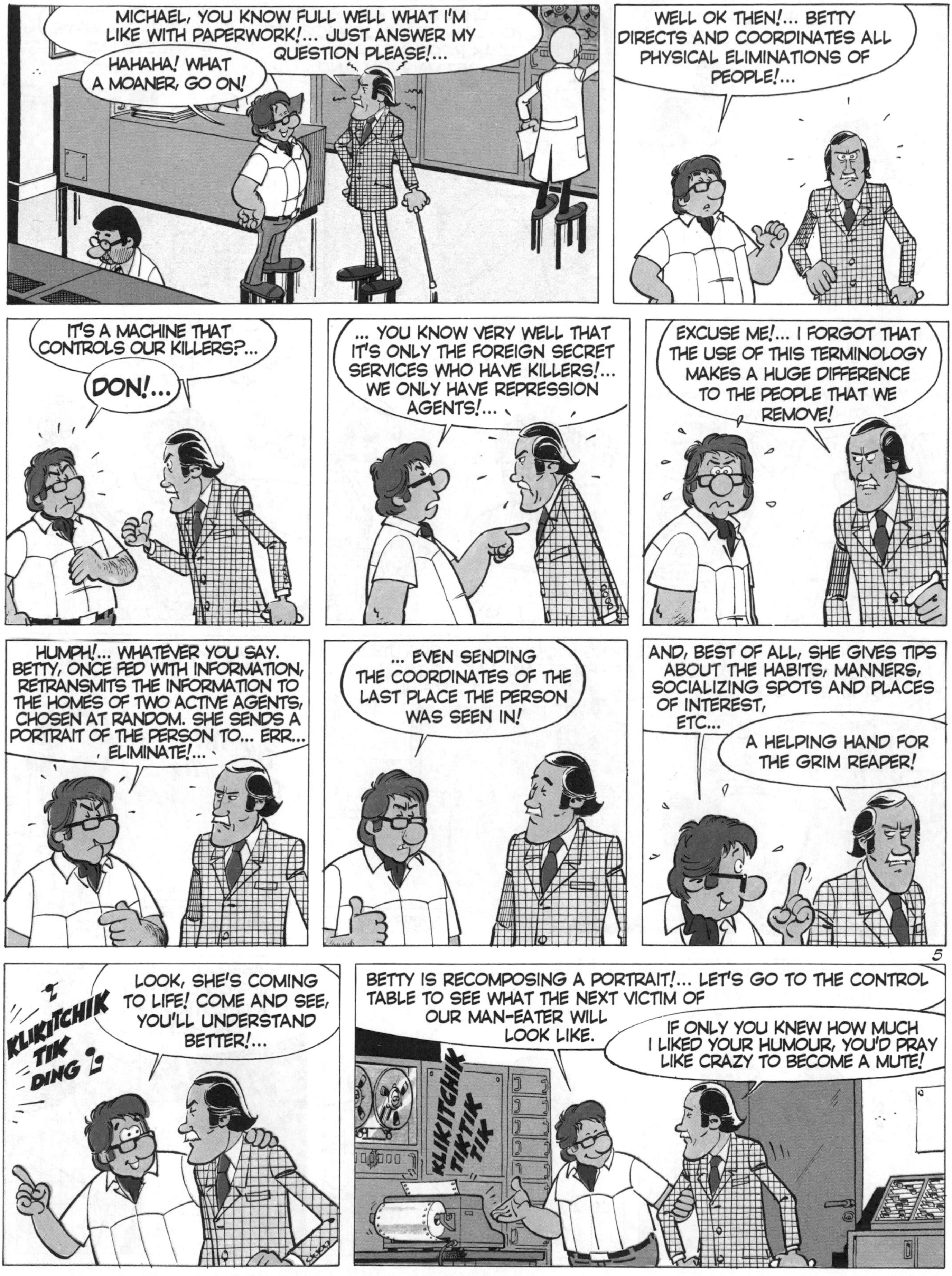
MICHAEL, YOU KNOW FULL WELL WHAT I'M LIKE WITH PAPERWORK!... JUST ANSWER MY QUESTION PLEASE!...
HAHAHA! WHAT A MOANER, GO ON!
WELL OK THEN!... BETTY DIRECTS AND COORDINATES ALL PHYSICAL ELIMINATIONS OF PEOPLE!...
IT'S A MACHINE THAT CONTROLS OUR KILLERS?...
DON!...
... YOU KNOW VERY WELL THAT IT'S ONLY THE FOREIGN SECRET SERVICES WHO HAVE KILLERS!... WE ONLY HAVE REPRESSION AGENTS!...
EXCUSE ME!... I FORGOT THAT THE USE OF THIS TERMINOLOGY MAKES A HUGE DIFFERENCE TO THE PEOPLE THAT WE REMOVE!
HUMPH!... WHATEVER YOU SAY. BETTY, ONCE FED WITH INFORMATION, RETRANSMITS THE INFORMATION TO THE HOMES OF TWO ACTIVE AGENTS, CHOSEN AT RANDOM. SHE SENDS A PORTRAIT OF THE PERSON TO... ERR... ELIMINATE!...
... EVEN SENDING THE COORDINATES OF THE LAST PLACE THE PERSON WAS SEEN IN!
AND, BEST OF ALL, SHE GIVES TIPS ABOUT THE HABITS, MANNERS, SOCIALIZING SPOTS AND PLACES OF INTEREST, ETC...
A HELPING HAND FOR THE GRIM REAPER!
5
KLIKITCHIK TIK DING
LOOK, SHE'S COMING TO LIFE! COME AND SEE, YOU'LL UNDERSTAND BETTER!...
BETTY IS RECOMPOSING A PORTRAIT!... LET'S GO TO THE CONTROL TABLE TO SEE WHAT THE NEXT VICTIM OF OUR MAN-EATER WILL LOOK LIKE.
IF ONLY YOU KNEW HOW MUCH I LIKED YOUR HUMOUR, YOU'D PRAY LIKE CRAZY TO BECOME A MUTE!
KLIKITCHIK TIKTIK TIK

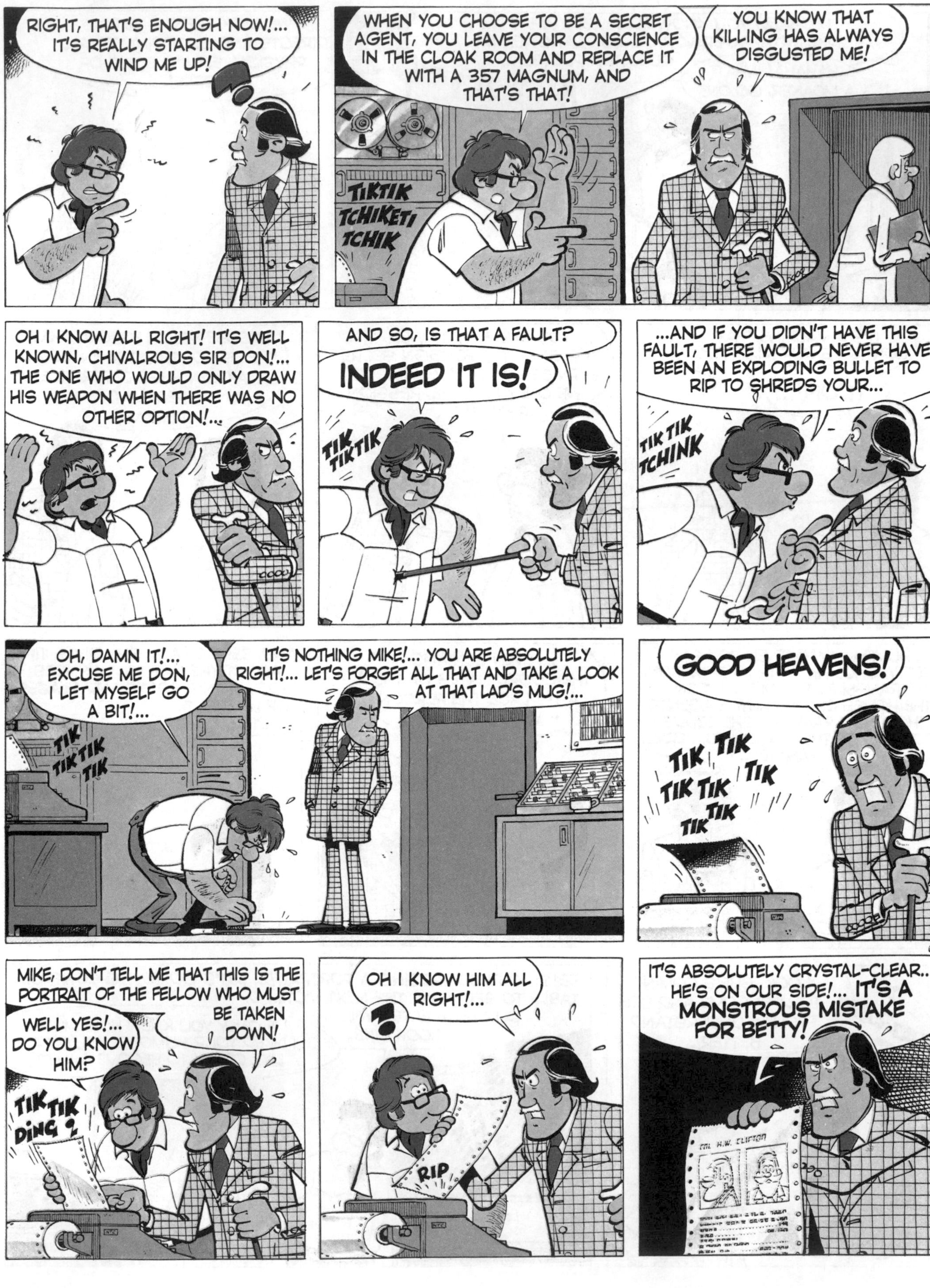
RIGHT, THAT'S ENOUGH NOW!... IT'S REALLY STARTING TO WIND ME UP!
WHEN YOU CHOOSE TO BE A SECRET AGENT, YOU LEAVE YOUR CONSCIENCE IN THE CLOAK ROOM AND REPLACE IT WITH A 357 MAGNUM, AND THAT'S THAT!
TIKTIK TCHIKETI TCHIK
YOU KNOW THAT KILLING HAS ALWAYS DISGUSTED ME!
OH I KNOW ALL RIGHT! IT'S WELL KNOWN, CHIVALROUS SIR DON!... THE ONE WHO WOULD ONLY DRAW HIS WEAPON WHEN THERE WAS NO OTHER OPTION!...
AND SO, IS THAT A FAULT?
INDEED IT IS!
TIK TIKTIK
...AND IF YOU DIDN'T HAVE THIS FAULT, THERE WOULD NEVER HAVE BEEN AN EXPLODING BULLET TO RIP TO SHREDS YOUR...
TIK TIK TCHINK
OH, DAMN IT!... EXCUSE ME DON, I LET MYSELF GO A BIT!...
IT'S NOTHING MIKE!... YOU ARE ABSOLUTELY RIGHT!... LET'S FORGET ALL THAT AND TAKE A LOOK AT THAT LAD'S MUG!...
TIK TIKTIK TIK
GOOD HEAVENS!
TIK TIK TIK TIK TIK TIK TIK
MIKE, DON'T TELL ME THAT THIS IS THE PORTRAIT OF THE FELLOW WHO MUST BE TAKEN DOWN!
WELL YES!... DO YOU KNOW HIM?
TIK TIK DING
OH I KNOW HIM ALL RIGHT!...
RIP
IT'S ABSOLUTELY CRYSTAL-CLEAR... HE'S ON OUR SIDE!... IT'S A MONSTROUS MISTAKE FOR BETTY!

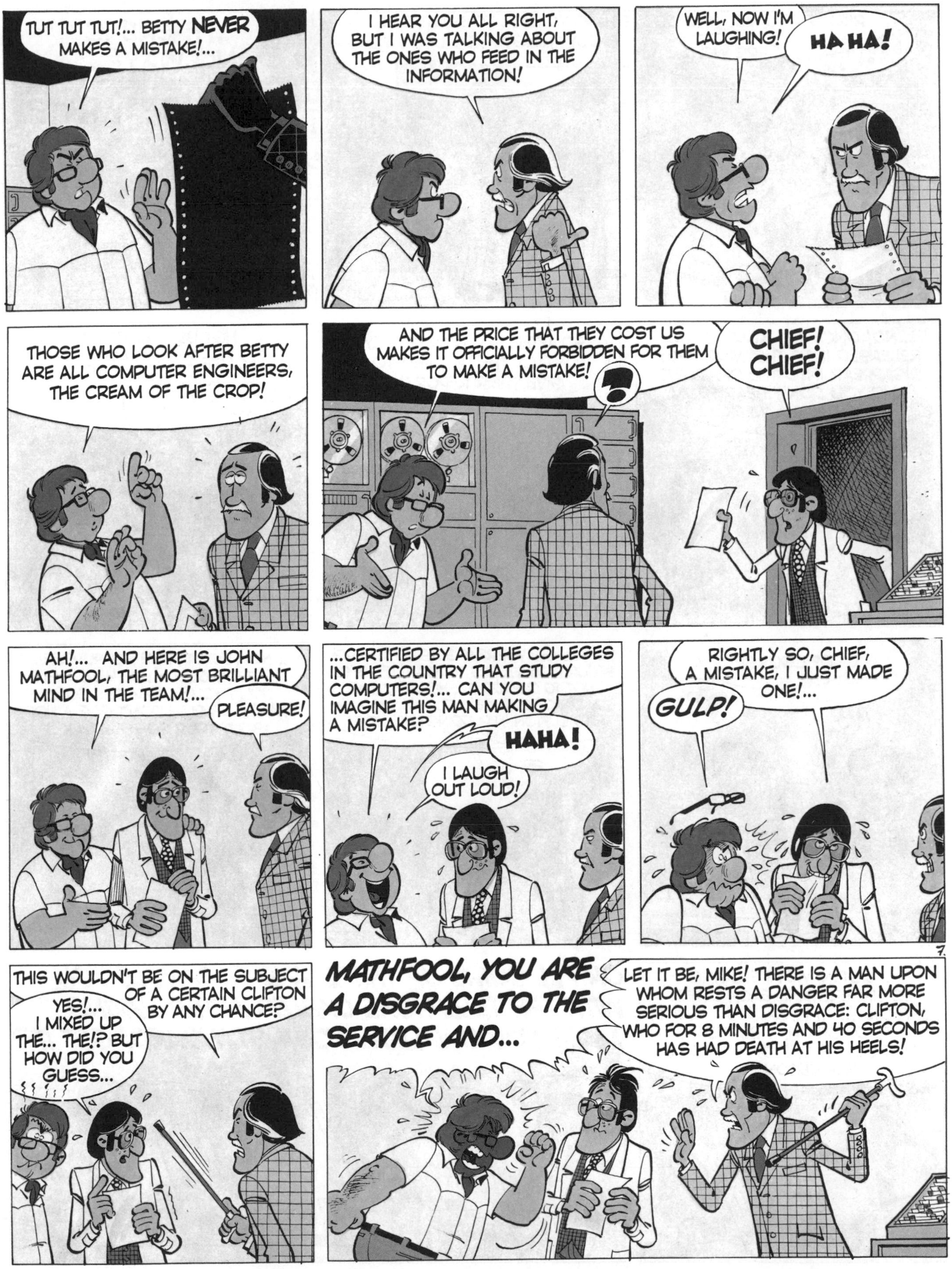
TUT TUT TUT!... BETTY NEVER MAKES A MISTAKE!...
I HEAR YOU ALL RIGHT, BUT I WAS TALKING ABOUT THE ONES WHO FEED IN THE INFORMATION!
WELL, NOW I'M LAUGHING!
HA HA!
THOSE WHO LOOK AFTER BETTY ARE ALL COMPUTER ENGINEERS, THE CREAM OF THE CROP!
AND THE PRICE THAT THEY COST US MAKES IT OFFICIALLY FORBIDDEN FOR THEM TO MAKE A MISTAKE!
CHIEF! CHIEF!
AH!... AND HERE IS JOHN MATHFOOL, THE MOST BRILLIANT MIND IN THE TEAM!...
PLEASURE!
...CERTIFIED BY ALL THE COLLEGES IN THE COUNTRY THAT STUDY COMPUTERS!... CAN YOU IMAGINE THIS MAN MAKING A MISTAKE?
HAHA!
I LAUGH OUT LOUD!
RIGHTLY SO, CHIEF, A MISTAKE, I JUST MADE ONE!...
GULP!
7.
THIS WOULDN'T BE ON THE SUBJECT OF A CERTAIN CLIFTON BY ANY CHANCE?
YES!... I MIXED UP THE... THE!? BUT HOW DID YOU GUESS...
MATHFOOL, YOU ARE A DISGRACE TO THE SERVICE AND...
LET IT BE, MIKE! THERE IS A MAN UPON WHOM RESTS A DANGER FAR MORE SERIOUS THAN DISGRACE: CLIFTON, WHO FOR 8 MINUTES AND 40 SECONDS HAS HAD DEATH AT HIS HEELS!

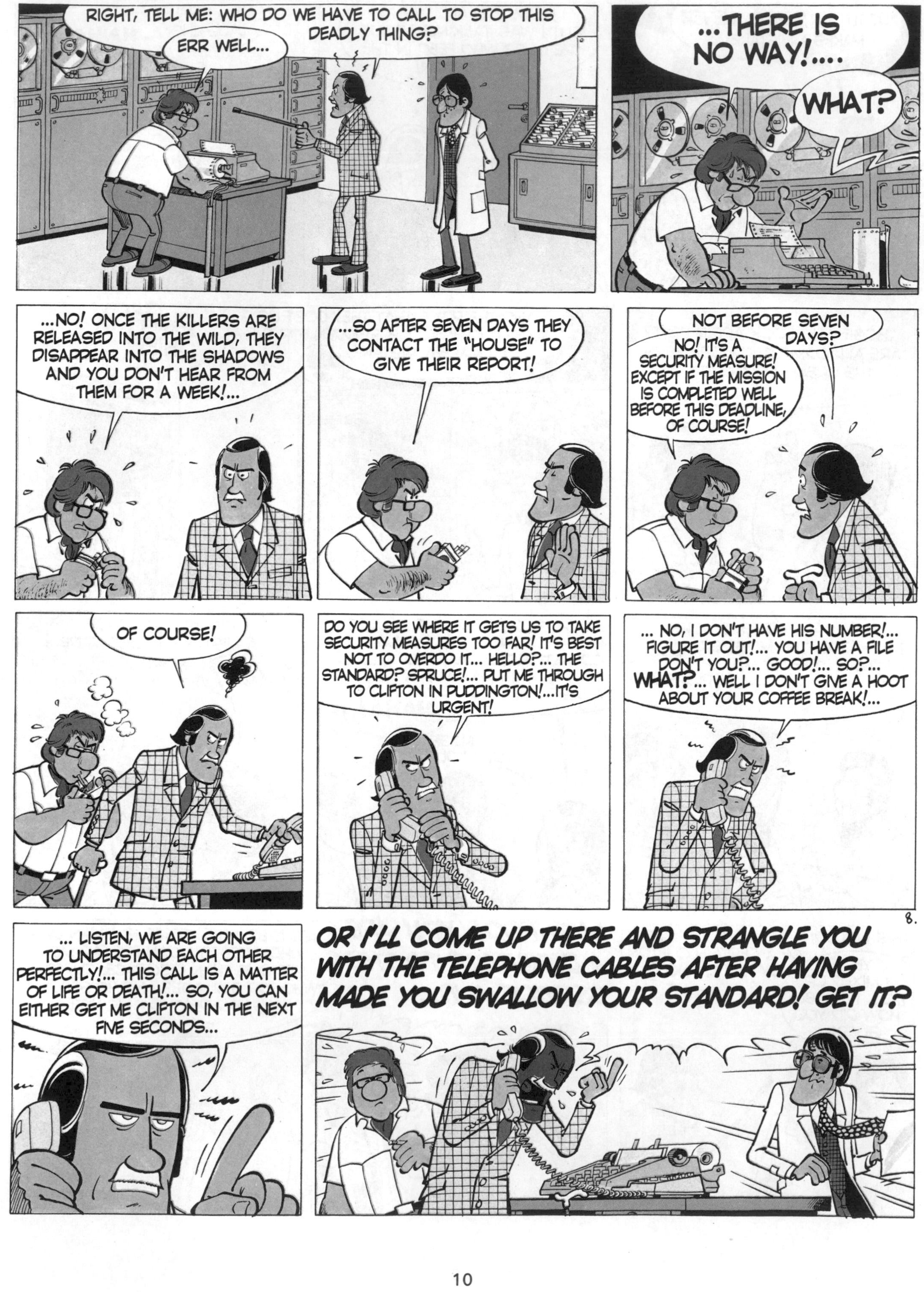
RIGHT, TELL ME: WHO DO WE HAVE TO CALL TO STOP THIS DEADLY THING?
ERR WELL...
...THERE IS NO WAY!....
WHAT?
...NO! ONCE THE KILLERS ARE RELEASED INTO THE WILD, THEY DISAPPEAR INTO THE SHADOWS AND YOU DON'T HEAR FROM THEM FOR A WEEK!...
...SO AFTER SEVEN DAYS THEY CONTACT THE "HOUSE" TO GIVE THEIR REPORT!
NOT BEFORE SEVEN DAYS?
NO! IT'S A SECURITY MEASURE! EXCEPT IF THE MISSION IS COMPLETED WELL BEFORE THIS DEADLINE, OF COURSE!
OF COURSE!
DO YOU SEE WHERE IT GETS US TO TAKE SECURITY MEASURES TOO FAR! IT'S BEST NOT TO OVERDO IT... HELLO?... THE STANDARD? SPRUCE!... PUT ME THROUGH TO CLIFTON IN PUDDINGTON!...IT'S URGENT!
... NO, I DON'T HAVE HIS NUMBER!... FIGURE IT OUT!... YOU HAVE A FILE DON'T YOU?... GOOD!... SO?... WHAT?... WELL I DON'T GIVE A HOOT ABOUT YOUR COFFEE BREAK!...
... LISTEN, WE ARE GOING TO UNDERSTAND EACH OTHER PERFECTLY!... THIS CALL IS A MATTER OF LIFE OR DEATH!... SO, YOU CAN EITHER GET ME CLIFTON IN THE NEXT FIVE SECONDS...
OR I'LL COME UP THERE AND STRANGLE YOU WITH THE TELEPHONE CABLES AFTER HAVING MADE YOU SWALLOW YOUR STANDARD! GET IT?

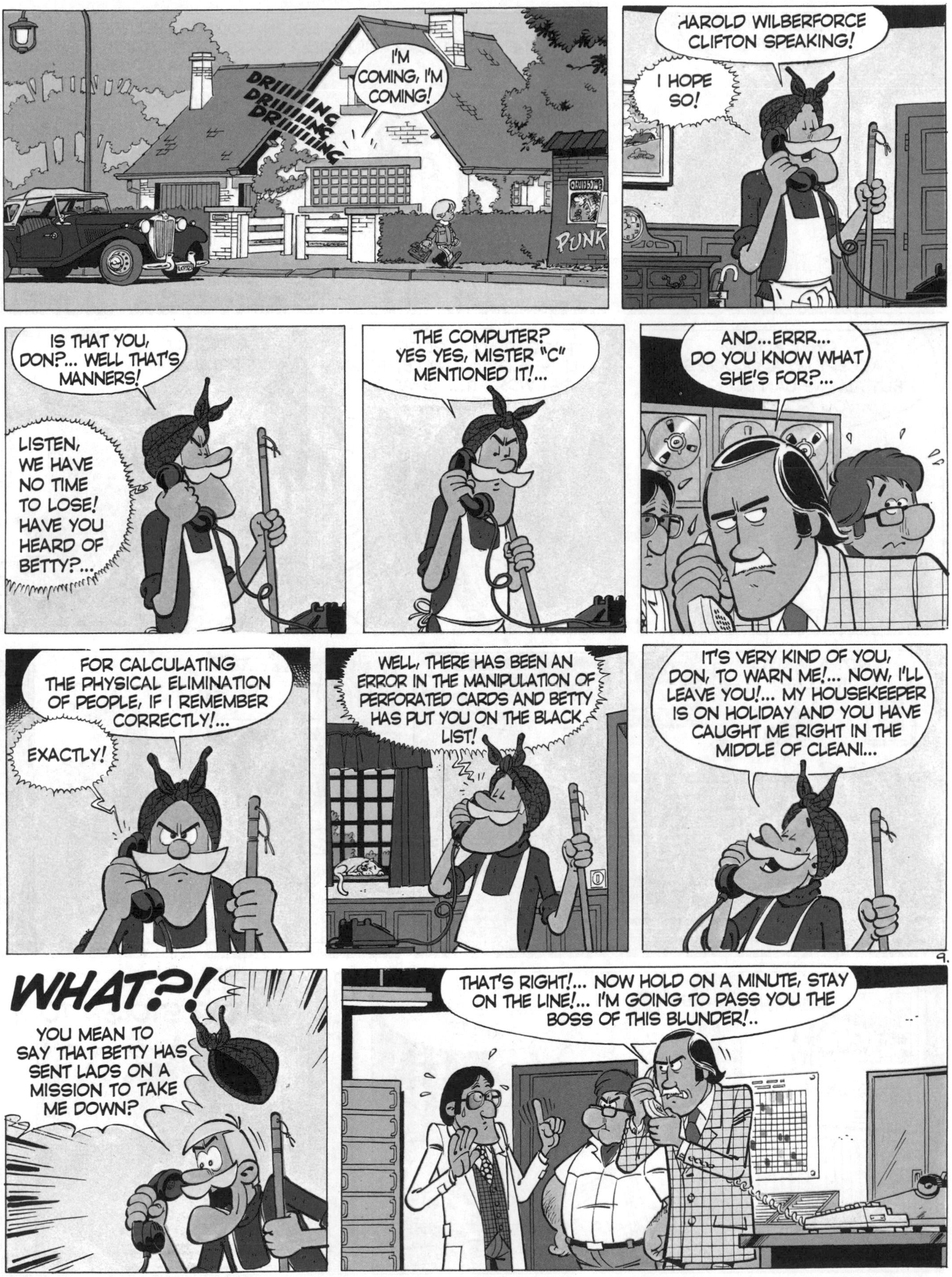
DRIIIIIIING DRIIIIIIING DRIIIIIIING
I'M COMING, I'M COMING!
PUNK
HAROLD WILBERFORCE CLIFTON SPEAKING!
I HOPE SO!
IS THAT YOU, DON?... WELL THAT'S MANNERS!
LISTEN, WE HAVE NO TIME TO LOSE! HAVE YOU HEARD OF BETTY?...
THE COMPUTER? YES YES, MISTER "C" MENTIONED IT!...
AND...ERRR... DO YOU KNOW WHAT SHE'S FOR?...
FOR CALCULATING THE PHYSICAL ELIMINATION OF PEOPLE, IF I REMEMBER CORRECTLY!...
EXACTLY!
WELL, THERE HAS BEEN AN ERROR IN THE MANIPULATION OF PERFORATED CARDS AND BETTY HAS PUT YOU ON THE BLACK LIST!
IT'S VERY KIND OF YOU, DON, TO WARN ME!... NOW, I'LL LEAVE YOU!... MY HOUSEKEEPER IS ON HOLIDAY AND YOU HAVE CAUGHT ME RIGHT IN THE MIDDLE OF CLEANI...
9.
WHAT?!
YOU MEAN TO SAY THAT BETTY HAS SENT LADS ON A MISSION TO TAKE ME DOWN?
THAT'S RIGHT!... NOW HOLD ON A MINUTE, STAY ON THE LINE!... I'M GOING TO PASS YOU THE BOSS OF THIS BLUNDER!..

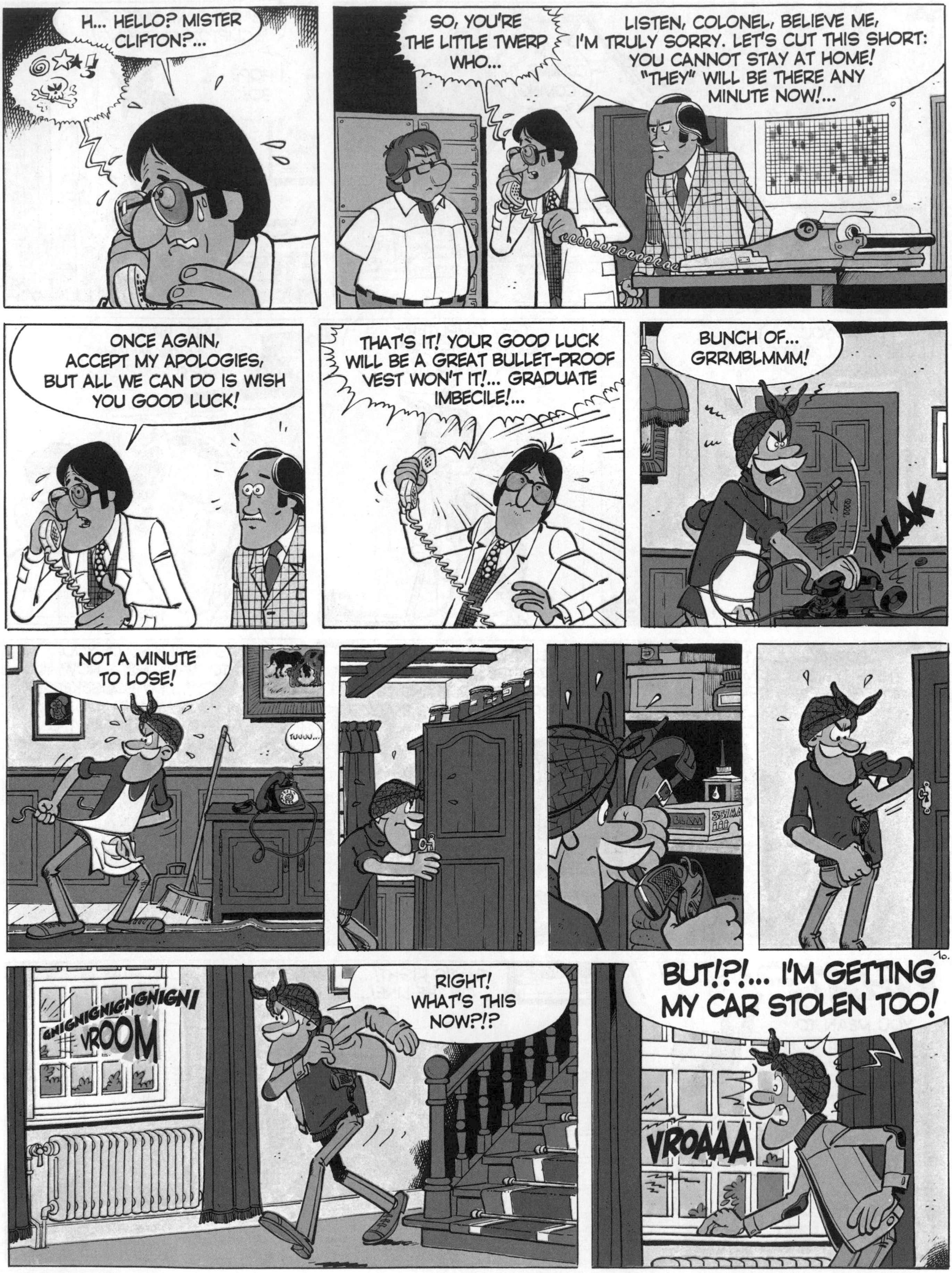
H... HELLO? MISTER CLIFTON?...
SO, YOU'RE THE LITTLE TWERP WHO...
LISTEN, COLONEL, BELIEVE ME, I'M TRULY SORRY. LET'S CUT THIS SHORT: YOU CANNOT STAY AT HOME! "THEY" WILL BE THERE ANY MINUTE NOW!...
ONCE AGAIN, ACCEPT MY APOLOGIES, BUT ALL WE CAN DO IS WISH YOU GOOD LUCK!
THAT'S IT! YOUR GOOD LUCK WILL BE A GREAT BULLET-PROOF VEST WON'T IT!... GRADUATE IMBECILE!...
BUNCH OF... GRRMBLMMM!
KLAK
NOT A MINUTE TO LOSE!
TUUUU...
GNIGNIGNIGNGNIGNI
VROOM
RIGHT! WHAT'S THIS NOW?!?
BUT!?!... I'M GETTING MY CAR STOLEN TOO!
VROAAA

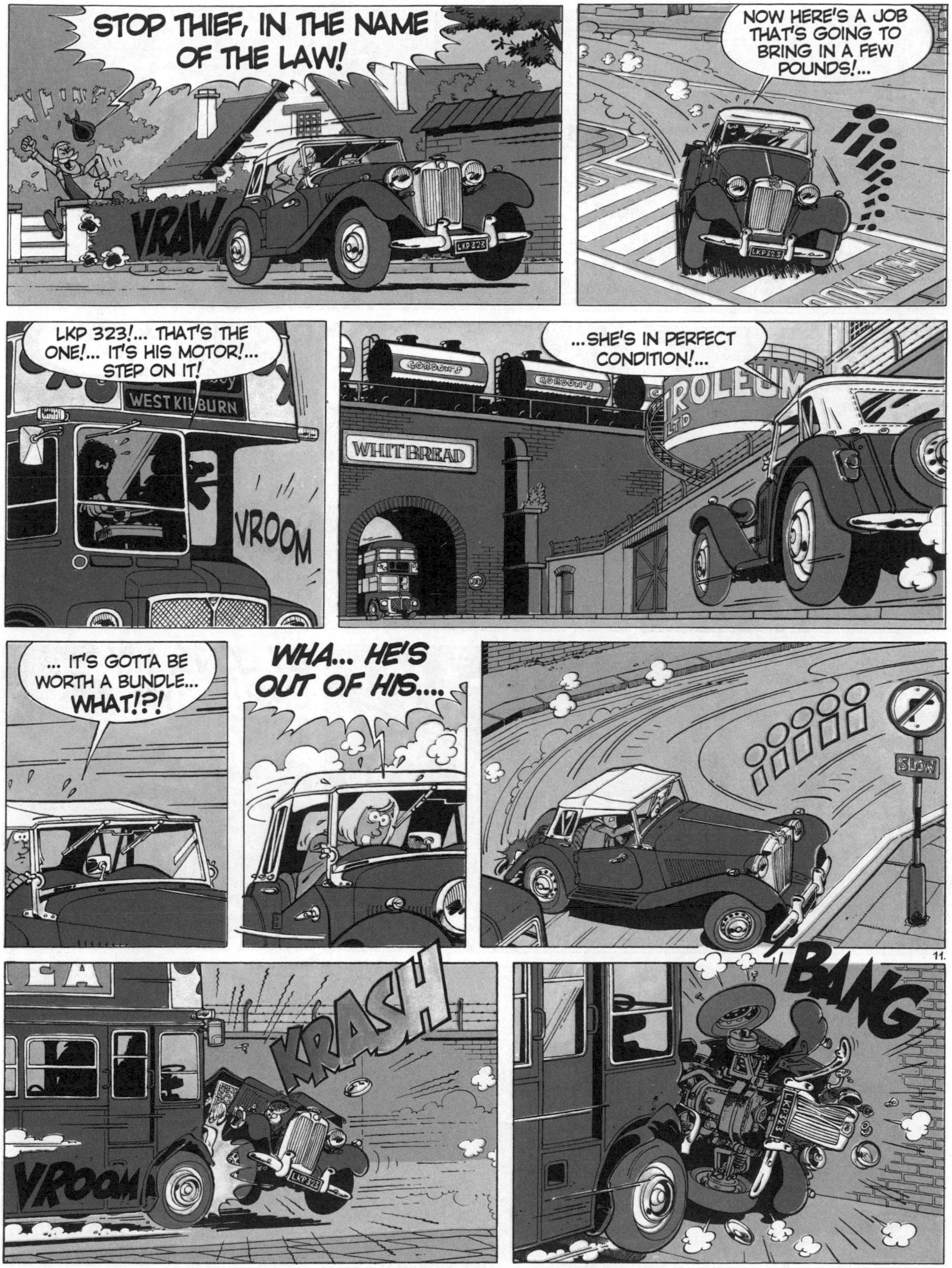
STOP THIEF, IN THE NAME OF THE LAW!
VRAW
NOW HERE'S A JOB THAT'S GOING TO BRING IN A FEW POUNDS!...
LKP 323!... THAT'S THE ONE!... IT'S HIS MOTOR!... STEP ON IT!
WEST KILBURN
VROOM
...SHE'S IN PERFECT CONDITION!...
WHITBREAD
... IT'S GOTTA BE WORTH A BUNDLE... WHAT!?!
WHA... HE'S OUT OF HIS....
SLOW
KRASH
VROOM
BANG

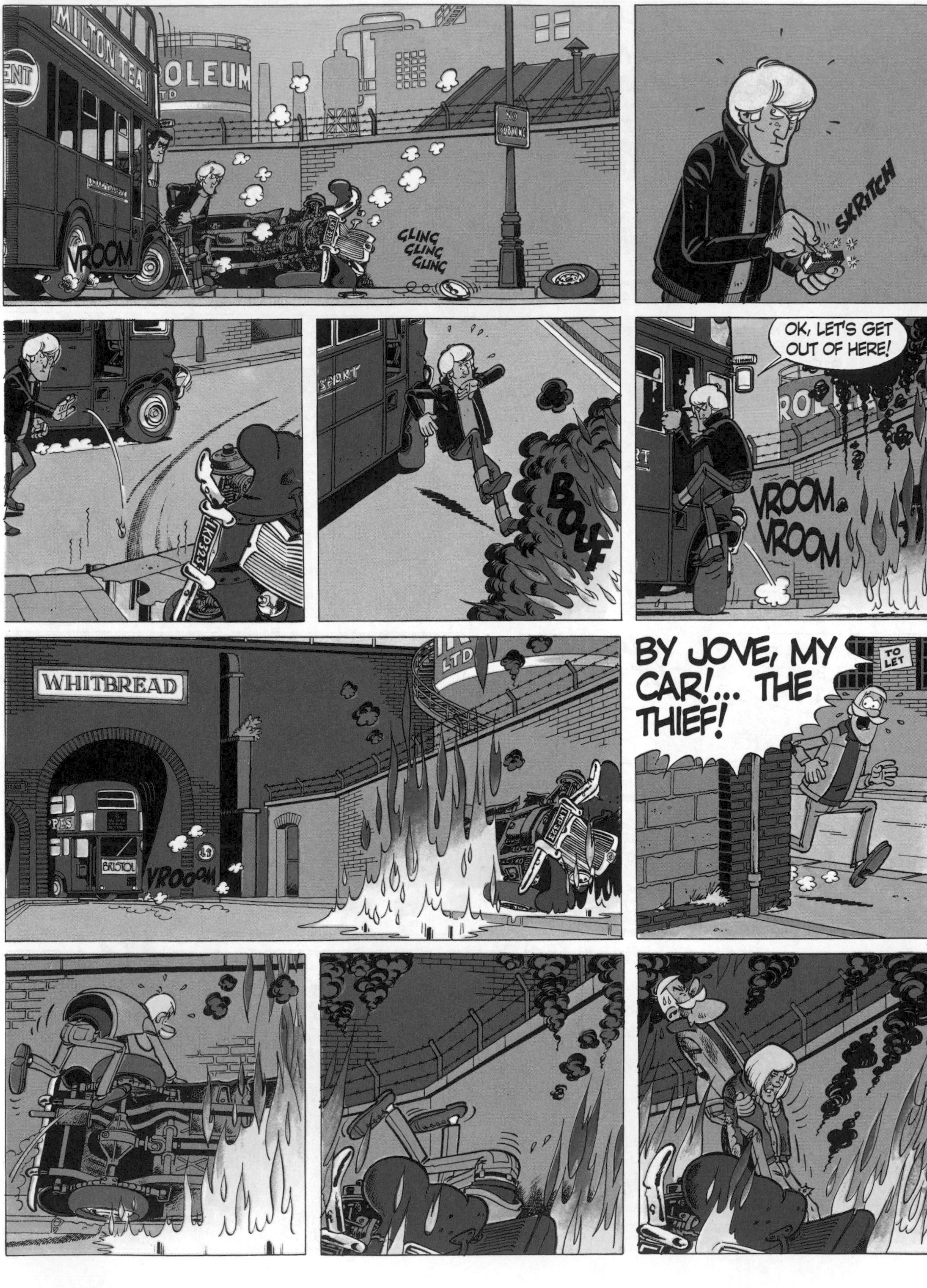

MILTON TEA
OLEUM
NO PARKING
VROOM
CLING CLING CLING
SKRITCH
BOUF
OK, LET'S GET OUT OF HERE!
VROOM VROOM
WHITBREAD
BRISTOL
VROOOM
BY JOVE, MY CAR!... THE THIEF!
TO LET

QUICK, IT COULD EXPL...

VOOOM

GOOD, THE LAD IS OUT OF DANGER, BUT NOT ME!

NO DOUBT ABOUT IT, THAT WAS ME THEY WERE AIMING FOR! FROM NOW ON I AM A MARKED MAN!...

"THEY" WILL SOON DISCOVER THAT IT WASN'T ME AT THE WHEEL OF THE M.G.!...

THAT LEAVES ME JUST ENOUGH TIME TO FLEE AND HIDE!...

LUCKILY I HAVE A PLACE IN LONDON!

... I WASN'T FOLLOWED, PERFECT!...

VROOM

GREAT IDEA OF MINE TO RENT OUT THIS STUDIO TO AVOID THE RETURN JOURNEY TO PUDDINGTON WHEN I HAVE BUSINESS IN TOWN!...

HELLO, COLONEL!

13.

15

MI...MISS MEDDING!

DID I SCARE YOU COLONEL? ... YOU SEEM A LITTLE SCARED!

YOU COULD SAY IT LOOKS LIKE YOU'VE GOT THE DEVIL AT YOUR HEELS!

NOT UNTRUE...

BUT, ALLOW ME TO INTRODUCE YOU TO MISS PALISH, MY BEST FRIEND!

HOW DO YOU DO?

TEEHEE!

SHE IS A FINE COOK... AND SINGLE... OLD DEVIL...

URP!

I... ERR... I'LL... UMM, WELL THERE WE GO, I'LL HAVE TO LEAVE YOU... ERR EXCUSE ME!...

TEEHEE, COLONEL!

PHEW!...FINALLY AT HOME!... WHAT A DAY!...

KLIK

I'D FORGOTTEN THAT MY LANDLADY HAD A MARITAL DISPOSITION!...

14.

MY GOD!... TEN TO FIVE!!! I NEARLY MISSED TEA-TIME!...

A GOOD CUP OF TEA WITH A SLICE OF CAKE, THAT'LL HELP ME TO FOCUS!

GOOD GRIEF, HOW!?!...

CHHHH

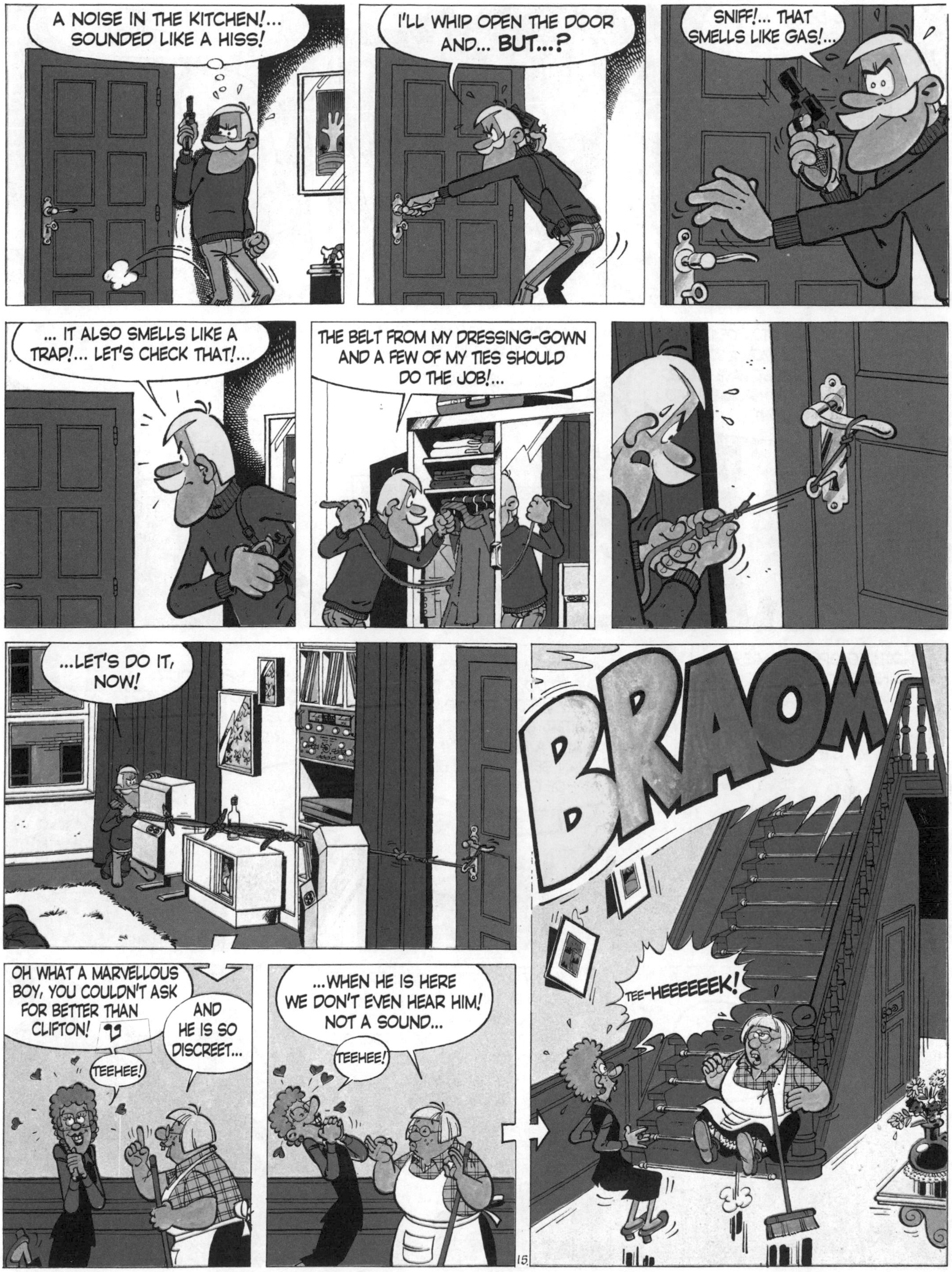
A NOISE IN THE KITCHEN!... SOUNDED LIKE A HISS!
I'LL WHIP OPEN THE DOOR AND... BUT...?
SNIFF!... THAT SMELLS LIKE GAS!...
... IT ALSO SMELLS LIKE A TRAP!... LET'S CHECK THAT!...
THE BELT FROM MY DRESSING-GOWN AND A FEW OF MY TIES SHOULD DO THE JOB!...
...LET'S DO IT, NOW!
OH WHAT A MARVELLOUS BOY, YOU COULDN'T ASK FOR BETTER THAN CLIFTON!
TEEHEE!
AND HE IS SO DISCREET...
...WHEN HE IS HERE WE DON'T EVEN HEAR HIM! NOT A SOUND...
TEEHEE!
BRAOM
TEE-HEEEEEEK!
15

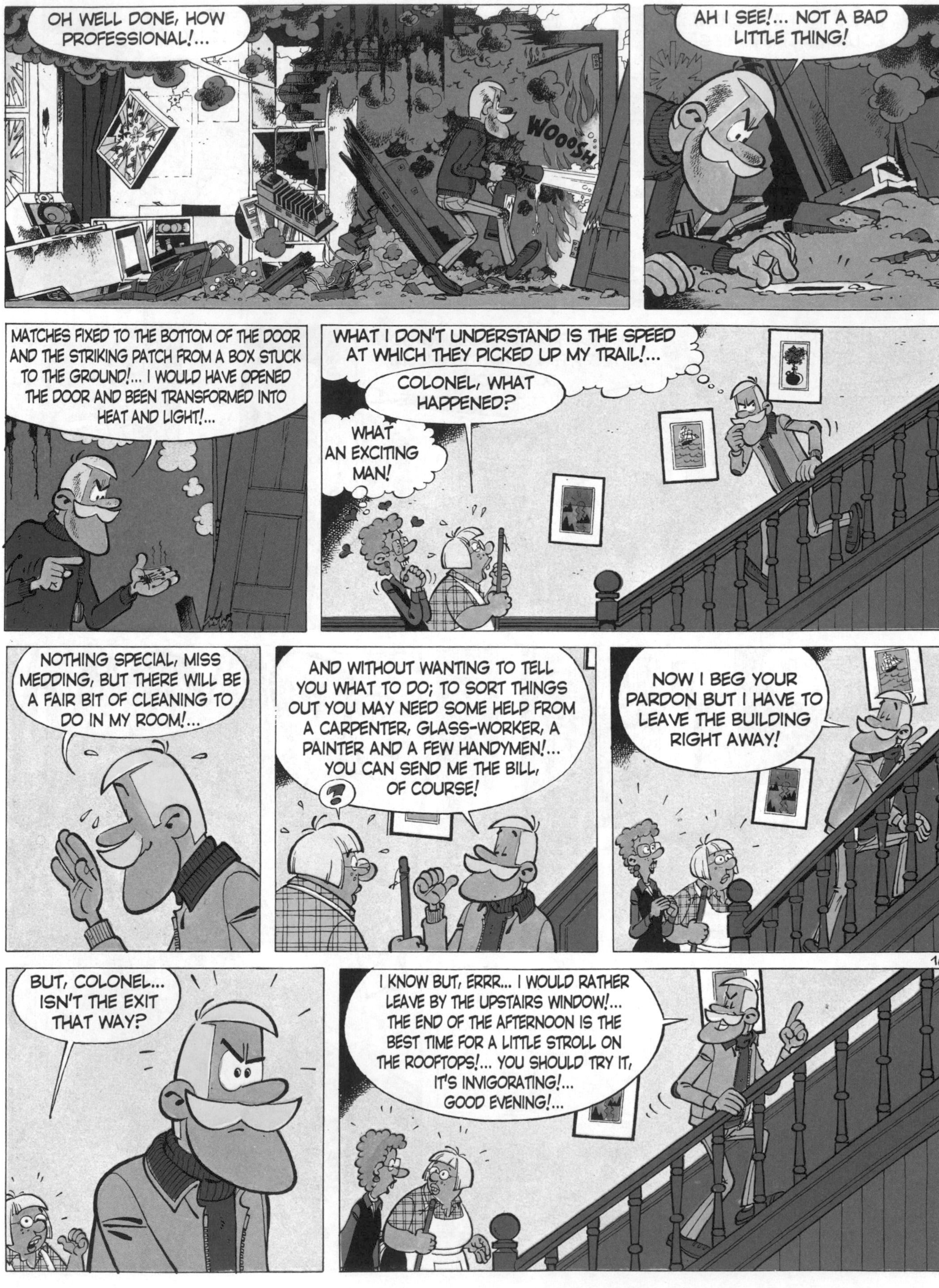
OH WELL DONE, HOW PROFESSIONAL!...
WOOOSH
AH I SEE!... NOT A BAD LITTLE THING!
MATCHES FIXED TO THE BOTTOM OF THE DOOR AND THE STRIKING PATCH FROM A BOX STUCK TO THE GROUND!... I WOULD HAVE OPENED THE DOOR AND BEEN TRANSFORMED INTO HEAT AND LIGHT!...
WHAT I DON'T UNDERSTAND IS THE SPEED AT WHICH THEY PICKED UP MY TRAIL!...
COLONEL, WHAT HAPPENED?
WHAT AN EXCITING MAN!
NOTHING SPECIAL, MISS MEDDING, BUT THERE WILL BE A FAIR BIT OF CLEANING TO DO IN MY ROOM!...
AND WITHOUT WANTING TO TELL YOU WHAT TO DO; TO SORT THINGS OUT YOU MAY NEED SOME HELP FROM A CARPENTER, GLASS-WORKER, A PAINTER AND A FEW HANDYMEN!... YOU CAN SEND ME THE BILL, OF COURSE!
NOW I BEG YOUR PARDON BUT I HAVE TO LEAVE THE BUILDING RIGHT AWAY!
16.
BUT, COLONEL... ISN'T THE EXIT THAT WAY?
I KNOW BUT, ERRR... I WOULD RATHER LEAVE BY THE UPSTAIRS WINDOW!... THE END OF THE AFTERNOON IS THE BEST TIME FOR A LITTLE STROLL ON THE ROOFTOPS!... YOU SHOULD TRY IT, IT'S INVIGORATING!... GOOD EVENING!...

BEING A BOY SCOUT IS COMING IN HANDY ONCE AGAIN!... KEEPS ME ON FORM!

OBVIOUSLY WHAT I'M DOING NOW HAS NOTHING TO DO WITH THE GAMES I PLAYED WHEN I WAS IN THE CUBS!

...ONE FALSE MOVE AND THE KILLERS WILL BE OUT OF WORK!...

HERE, THIS WILL DO!

...HERE'S HOPING THAT THE CONCIERGE WON'T BE IN THE STAIRWELL...

KLING!

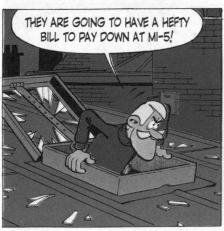

THEY ARE GOING TO HAVE A HEFTY BILL TO PAY DOWN AT MI-5!

ALL I HAVE TO DO NOW IS LEAVE DISCREETLY!

STOP! DON'T MOVE!

...YOU DON'T LIVE HERE! ...WHAT DO YOU WANT?

ERRR!... IT WAS FOR... ERR... MISTER SMITH....ERRR.... ISN'T HE BACK YET?...

THERE'S NO SMITH HERE!

HE DOESN'T LIVE HERE?... AH, WELL THAT MUST BE WHY HE ISN'T BACK!... EXCUSE ME AND TAKE CARE!...

KRIOUI!!

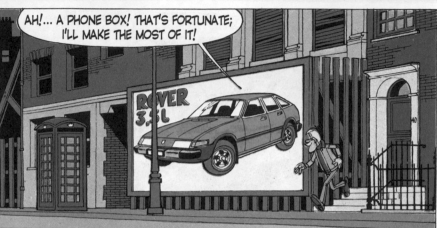

AH!... A PHONE BOX! THAT'S FORTUNATE; I'LL MAKE THE MOST OF IT!

ROVER 3.5L

OF COURSE IT'S ME!... WHO DID YOU THINK IT WAS?

AND AS I'D LIKE TO SPEAK TO SOMEONE WITH AN IQ HIGHER THAN 2, GET OFF THE LINE AND PASS ME DON SPRUCE!

...BUT I TOLD YOU THAT THEY KNOW ALL OF YOUR HABITS!!!

BUT!?!... I NEVER GAVE THIS ADDRESS TO MI-5!?!...

WE DIDN'T NEED TO ASK YOU FOR IT, IT WAS ON FILE FROM THE MOMENT YOU WERE HIRED. WE KNOW EVERYTHING HERE, YOU KNOW...

OH!

EXCUSE ME, I'M HANGING UP! SOMEONE WOULD LIKE TO USE THE PHONE!

VROOOM

20

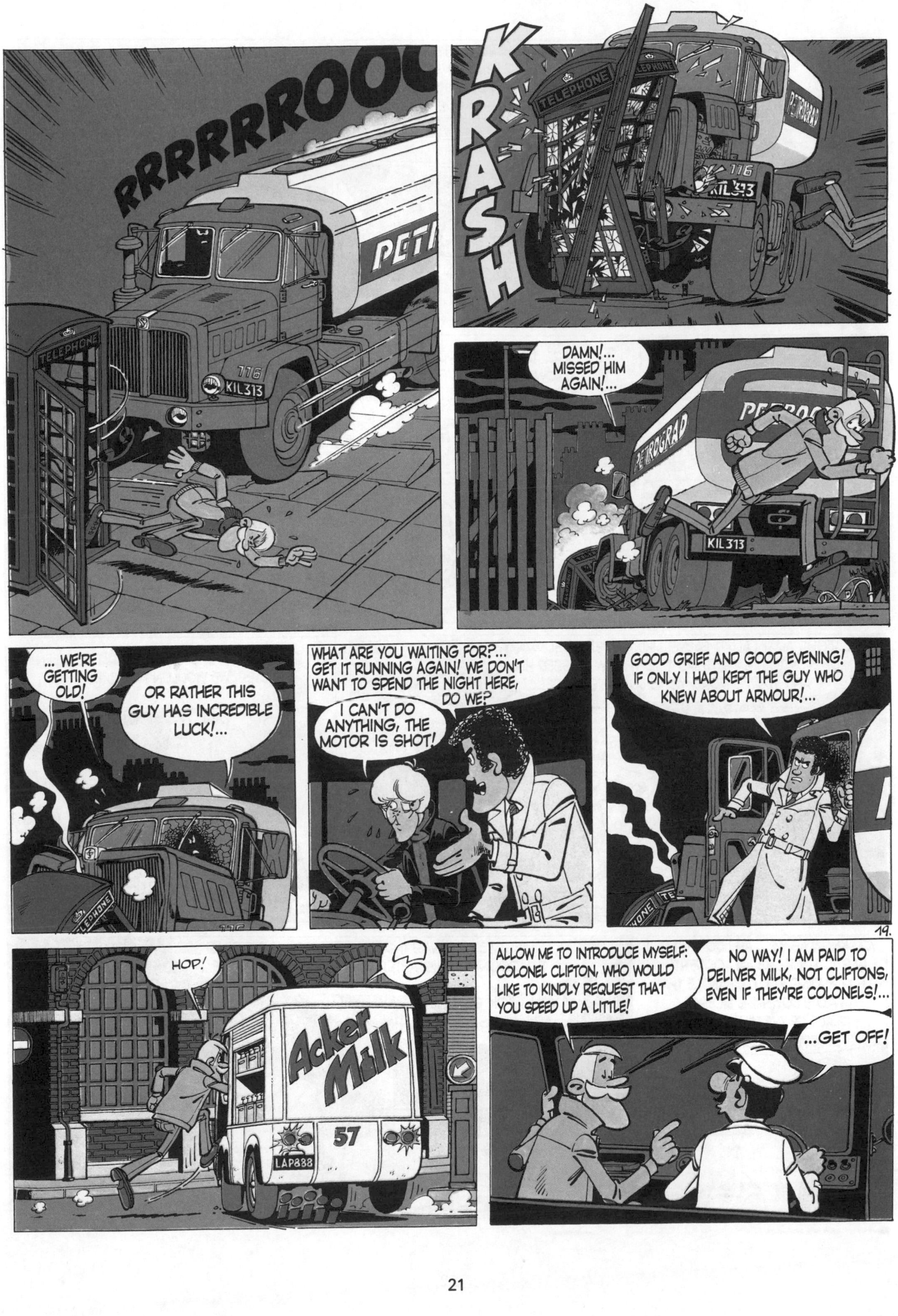
RRRRRROOO
KRASH
DAMN!... MISSED HIM AGAIN!...
... WE'RE GETTING OLD!
OR RATHER THIS GUY HAS INCREDIBLE LUCK!...
WHAT ARE YOU WAITING FOR?... GET IT RUNNING AGAIN! WE DON'T WANT TO SPEND THE NIGHT HERE, DO WE?
I CAN'T DO ANYTHING, THE MOTOR IS SHOT!
GOOD GRIEF AND GOOD EVENING! IF ONLY I HAD KEPT THE GUY WHO KNEW ABOUT ARMOUR!...
19.
HOP!
Acker Milk
ALLOW ME TO INTRODUCE MYSELF: COLONEL CLIFTON, WHO WOULD LIKE TO KINDLY REQUEST THAT YOU SPEED UP A LITTLE!
NO WAY! I AM PAID TO DELIVER MILK, NOT CLIFTONS, EVEN IF THEY'RE COLONELS!...
...GET OFF!

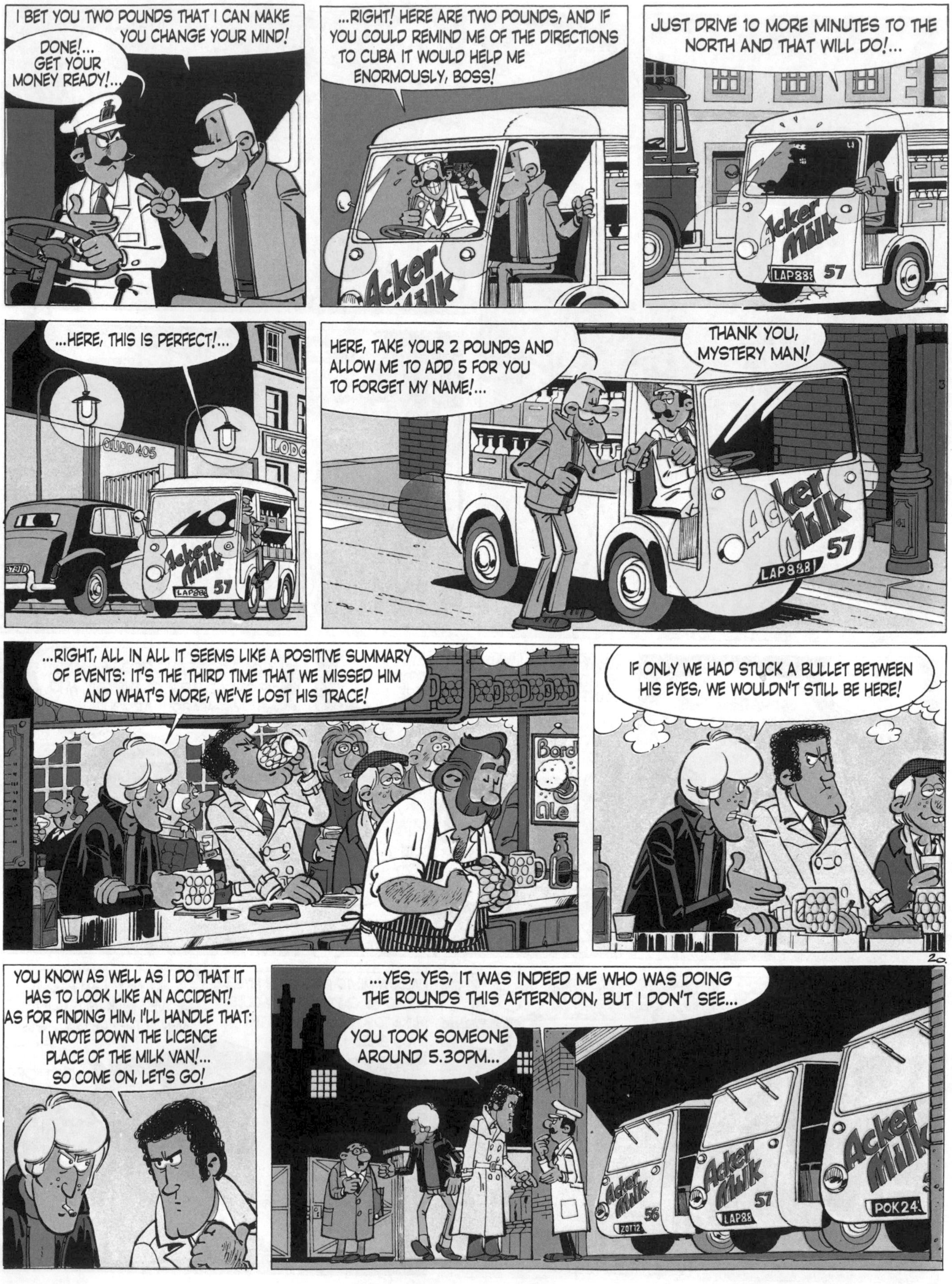
I BET YOU TWO POUNDS THAT I CAN MAKE YOU CHANGE YOUR MIND!
DONE!... GET YOUR MONEY READY!...
...RIGHT! HERE ARE TWO POUNDS, AND IF YOU COULD REMIND ME OF THE DIRECTIONS TO CUBA IT WOULD HELP ME ENORMOUSLY, BOSS!
JUST DRIVE 10 MORE MINUTES TO THE NORTH AND THAT WILL DO!...
...HERE, THIS IS PERFECT!...
HERE, TAKE YOUR 2 POUNDS AND ALLOW ME TO ADD 5 FOR YOU TO FORGET MY NAME!...
THANK YOU, MYSTERY MAN!
...RIGHT, ALL IN ALL IT SEEMS LIKE A POSITIVE SUMMARY OF EVENTS: IT'S THE THIRD TIME THAT WE MISSED HIM AND WHAT'S MORE, WE'VE LOST HIS TRACE!
IF ONLY WE HAD STUCK A BULLET BETWEEN HIS EYES, WE WOULDN'T STILL BE HERE!
YOU KNOW AS WELL AS I DO THAT IT HAS TO LOOK LIKE AN ACCIDENT! AS FOR FINDING HIM, I'LL HANDLE THAT: I WROTE DOWN THE LICENCE PLACE OF THE MILK VAN!... SO COME ON, LET'S GO!
...YES, YES, IT WAS INDEED ME WHO WAS DOING THE ROUNDS THIS AFTERNOON, BUT I DON'T SEE...
YOU TOOK SOMEONE AROUND 5.30PM...

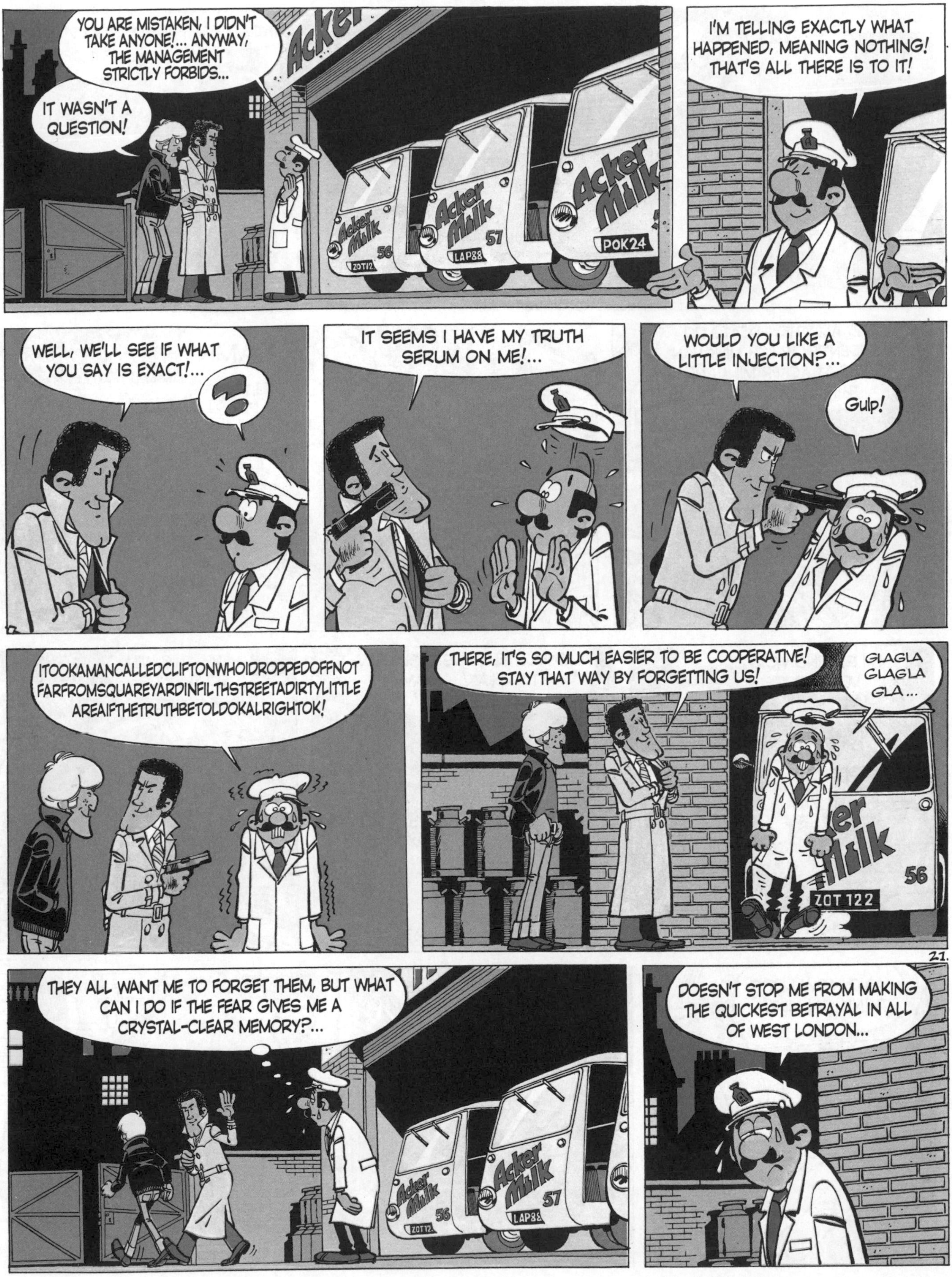
YOU ARE MISTAKEN, I DIDN'T TAKE ANYONE!... ANYWAY, THE MANAGEMENT STRICTLY FORBIDS...
IT WASN'T A QUESTION!
Acker
Acker Milk
I'M TELLING EXACTLY WHAT HAPPENED, MEANING NOTHING! THAT'S ALL THERE IS TO IT!
WELL, WE'LL SEE IF WHAT YOU SAY IS EXACT!...
IT SEEMS I HAVE MY TRUTH SERUM ON ME!...
WOULD YOU LIKE A LITTLE INJECTION?...
Gulp!
ITOOKAMANCALLEDCLIFTONWHOIDROPPEDOFFNOT FARFROMSQUAREYARDINFILTHSTREETADIRTYLITTLE AREAIFTHETRUTHBETOLDOKALRIGHTOK!
THERE, IT'S SO MUCH EASIER TO BE COOPERATIVE! STAY THAT WAY BY FORGETTING US!
GLAGLA GLAGLA GLA...
THEY ALL WANT ME TO FORGET THEM, BUT WHAT CAN I DO IF THE FEAR GIVES ME A CRYSTAL-CLEAR MEMORY?...
DOESN'T STOP ME FROM MAKING THE QUICKEST BETRAYAL IN ALL OF WEST LONDON...

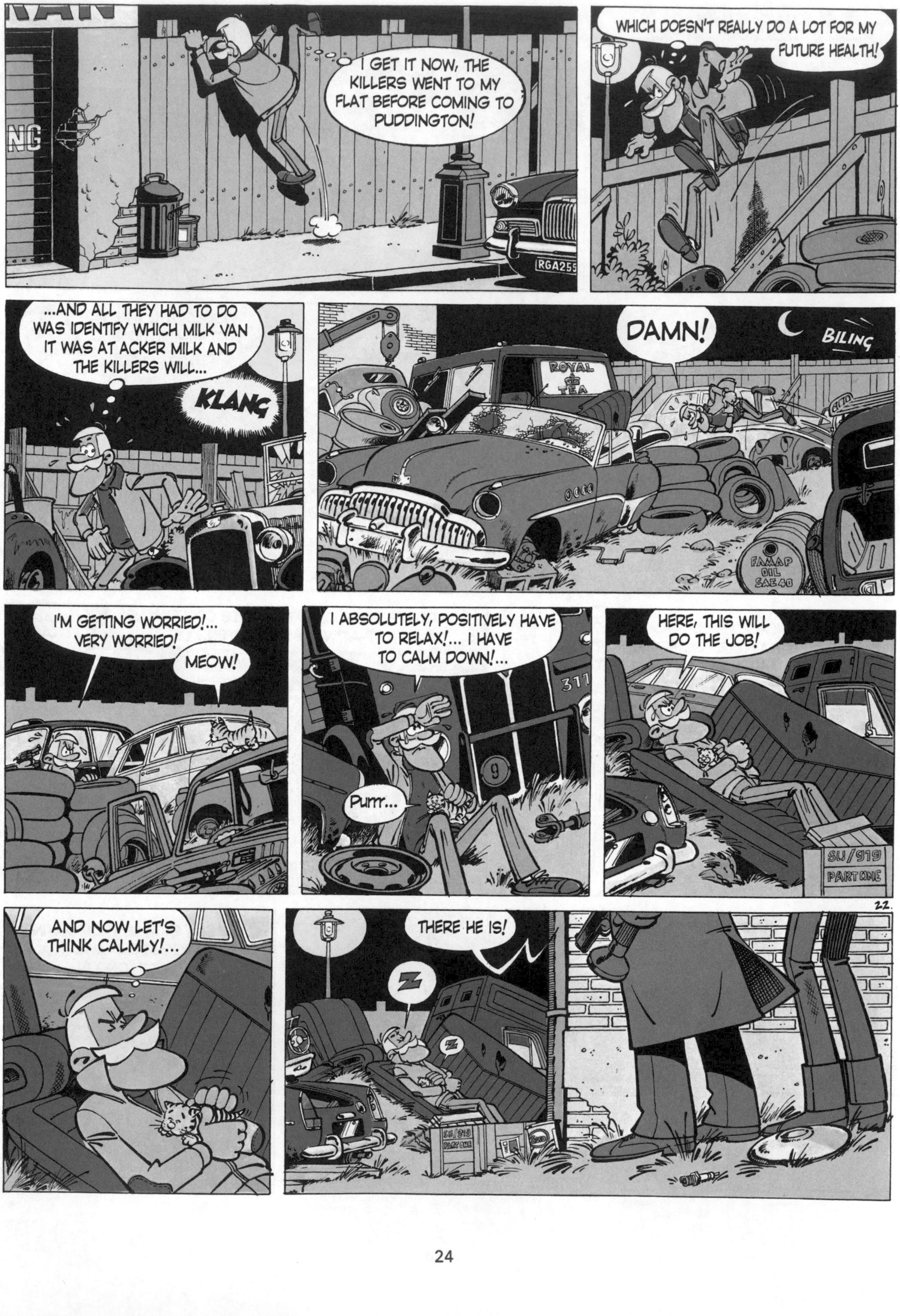
I GET IT NOW, THE KILLERS WENT TO MY FLAT BEFORE COMING TO PUDDINGTON!
RGA255
WHICH DOESN'T REALLY DO A LOT FOR MY FUTURE HEALTH!
...AND ALL THEY HAD TO DO WAS IDENTIFY WHICH MILK VAN IT WAS AT ACKER MILK AND THE KILLERS WILL...
KLANG
DAMN!
BILING
ROYAL TEA
FAMAP OIL SAE 40
I'M GETTING WORRIED!... VERY WORRIED!
MEOW!
I ABSOLUTELY, POSITIVELY HAVE TO RELAX!... I HAVE TO CALM DOWN!...
Purrr...
HERE, THIS WILL DO THE JOB!
SU/919 PART ONE
22.
AND NOW LET'S THINK CALMLY!...
THERE HE IS!
Z
Z

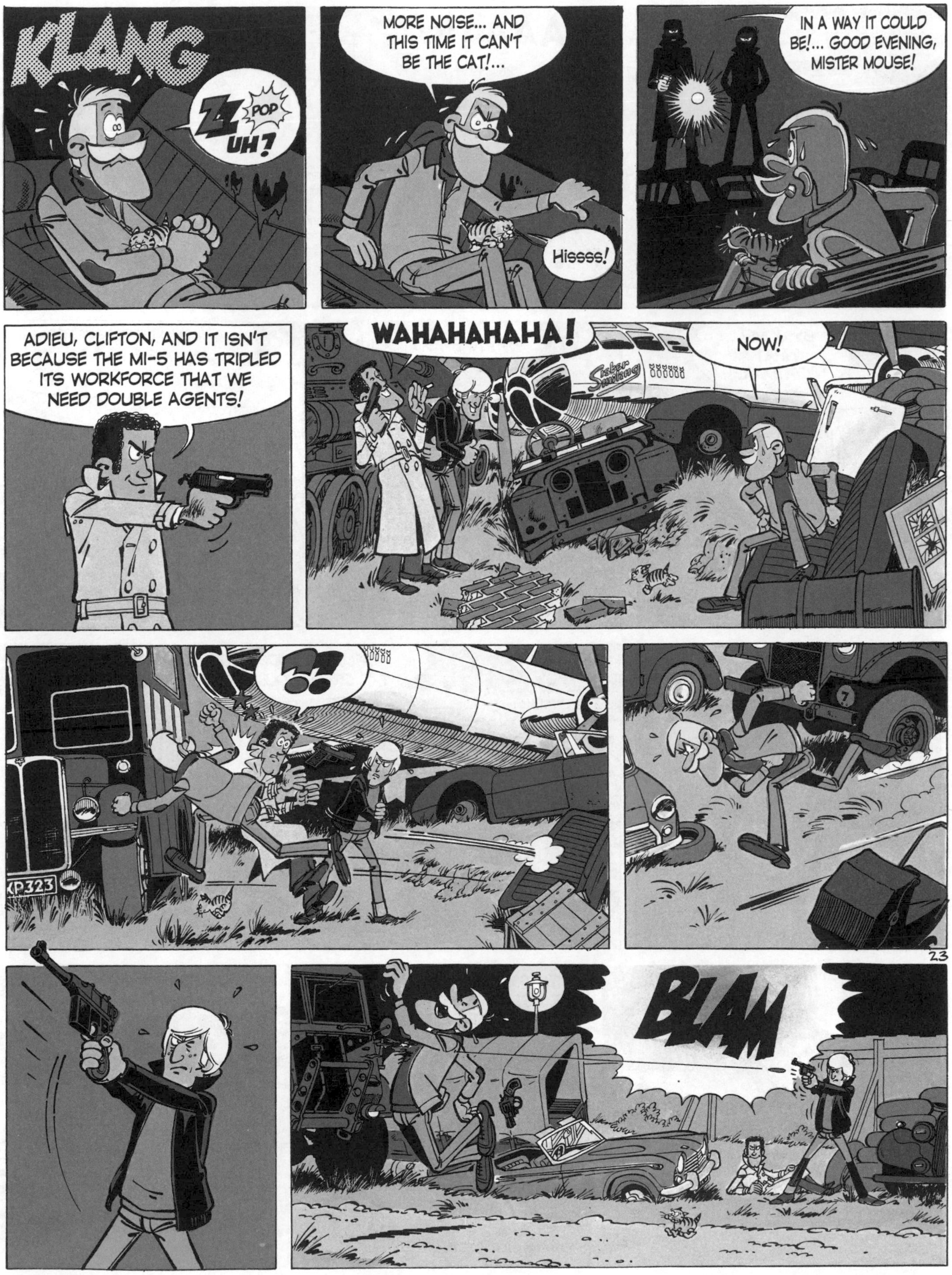
KLANG
ZZ
POP
UH?
MORE NOISE... AND THIS TIME IT CAN'T BE THE CAT!...
Hissss!
IN A WAY IT COULD BE!... GOOD EVENING, MISTER MOUSE!
ADIEU, CLIFTON, AND IT ISN'T BECAUSE THE MI-5 HAS TRIPLED ITS WORKFORCE THAT WE NEED DOUBLE AGENTS!
WAHAHAHAHA!
NOW!
KP323
BLAM

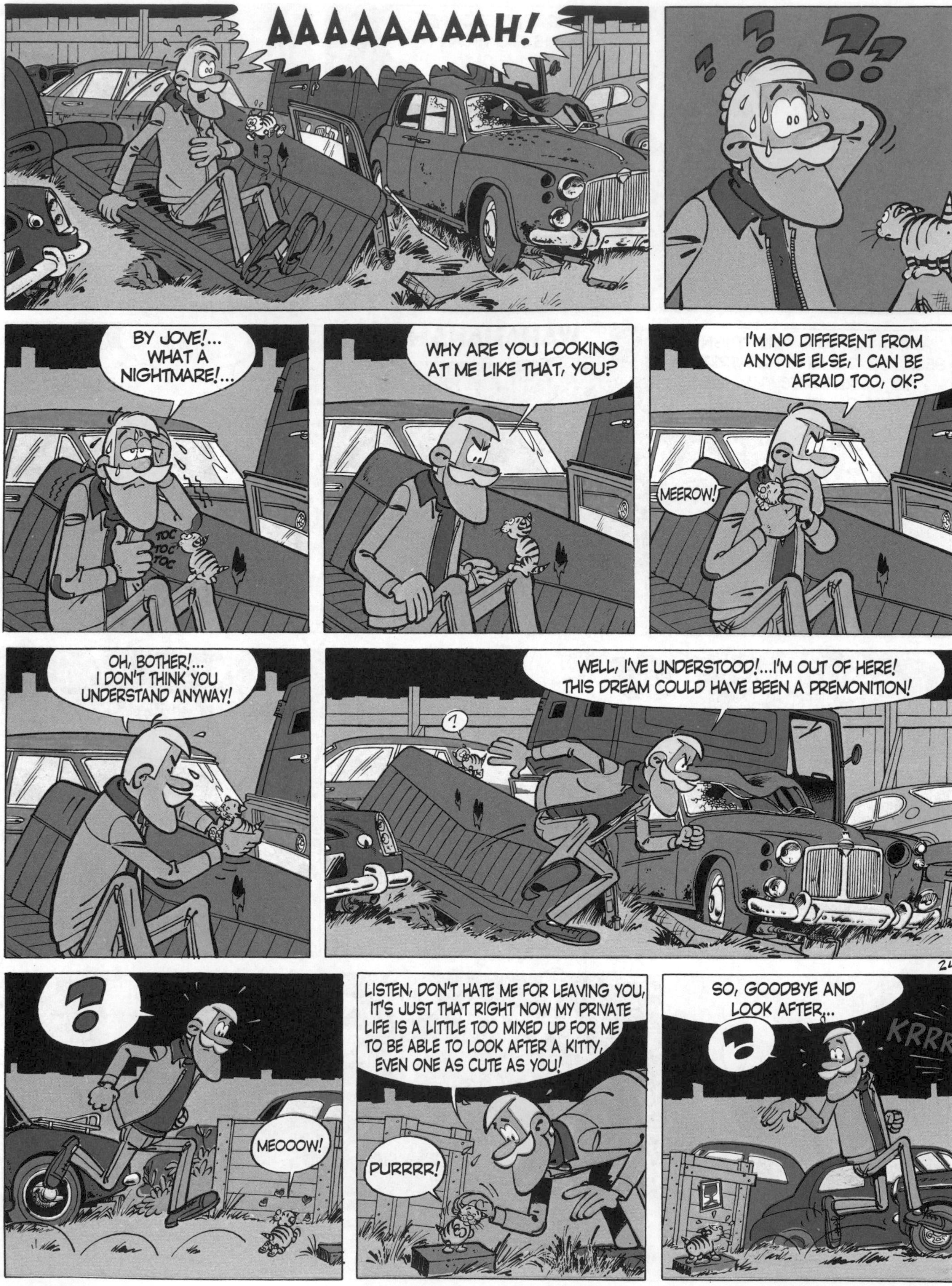
AAAAAAAAH!
BY JOVE!... WHAT A NIGHTMARE!...
TOC TOC TOC
WHY ARE YOU LOOKING AT ME LIKE THAT, YOU?
I'M NO DIFFERENT FROM ANYONE ELSE, I CAN BE AFRAID TOO, OK?
MEEROW!
OH, BOTHER!... I DON'T THINK YOU UNDERSTAND ANYWAY!
WELL, I'VE UNDERSTOOD!...I'M OUT OF HERE! THIS DREAM COULD HAVE BEEN A PREMONITION!
?
24.
MEOOOW!
LISTEN, DON'T HATE ME FOR LEAVING YOU, IT'S JUST THAT RIGHT NOW MY PRIVATE LIFE IS A LITTLE TOO MIXED UP FOR ME TO BE ABLE TO LOOK AFTER A KITTY, EVEN ONE AS CUTE AS YOU!
PURRRR!
SO, GOODBYE AND LOOK AFTER...
KRRR

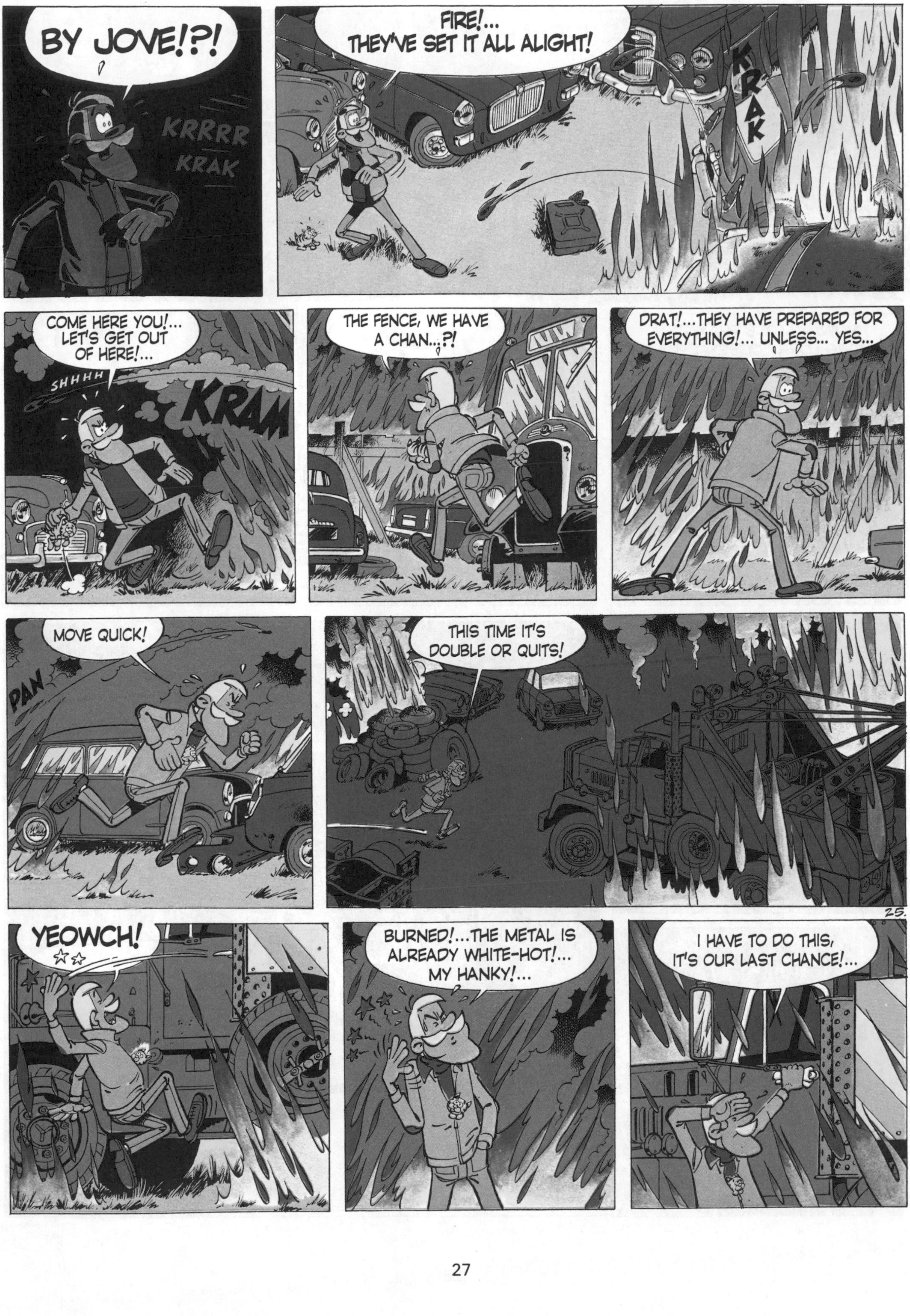

BY JOVE!?!
KRRRR
KRAK
FIRE!...
THEY'VE SET IT ALL ALIGHT!
KRAK
COME HERE YOU!...
LET'S GET OUT
OF HERE!...
SHHHH
KRAM
THE FENCE, WE HAVE
A CHAN...?!
DRAT!...THEY HAVE PREPARED FOR
EVERYTHING!... UNLESS... YES...
MOVE QUICK!
PAN
THIS TIME IT'S
DOUBLE OR QUITS!
25.
YEOWCH!
BURNED!...THE METAL IS
ALREADY WHITE-HOT!...
MY HANKY!...
I HAVE TO DO THIS,
IT'S OUR LAST CHANCE!...

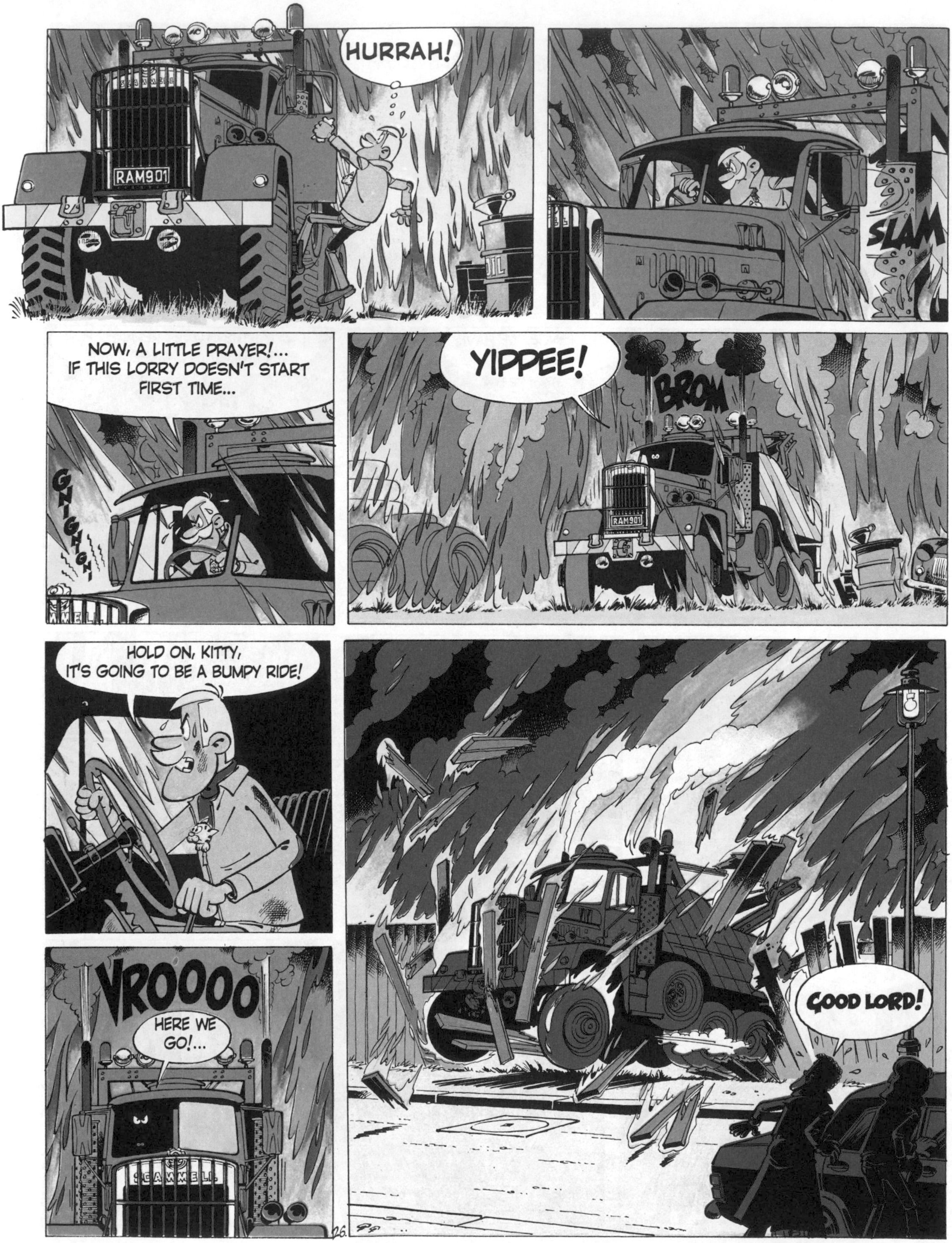
HURRAH!
RAM901
SLAM
NOW, A LITTLE PRAYER!... IF THIS LORRY DOESN'T START FIRST TIME...
GNIGNIGNI
YIPPEE!
BROM
RAM901
HOLD ON, KITTY, IT'S GOING TO BE A BUMPY RIDE!
VROOOO
HERE WE GO!...
GOOD LORD!

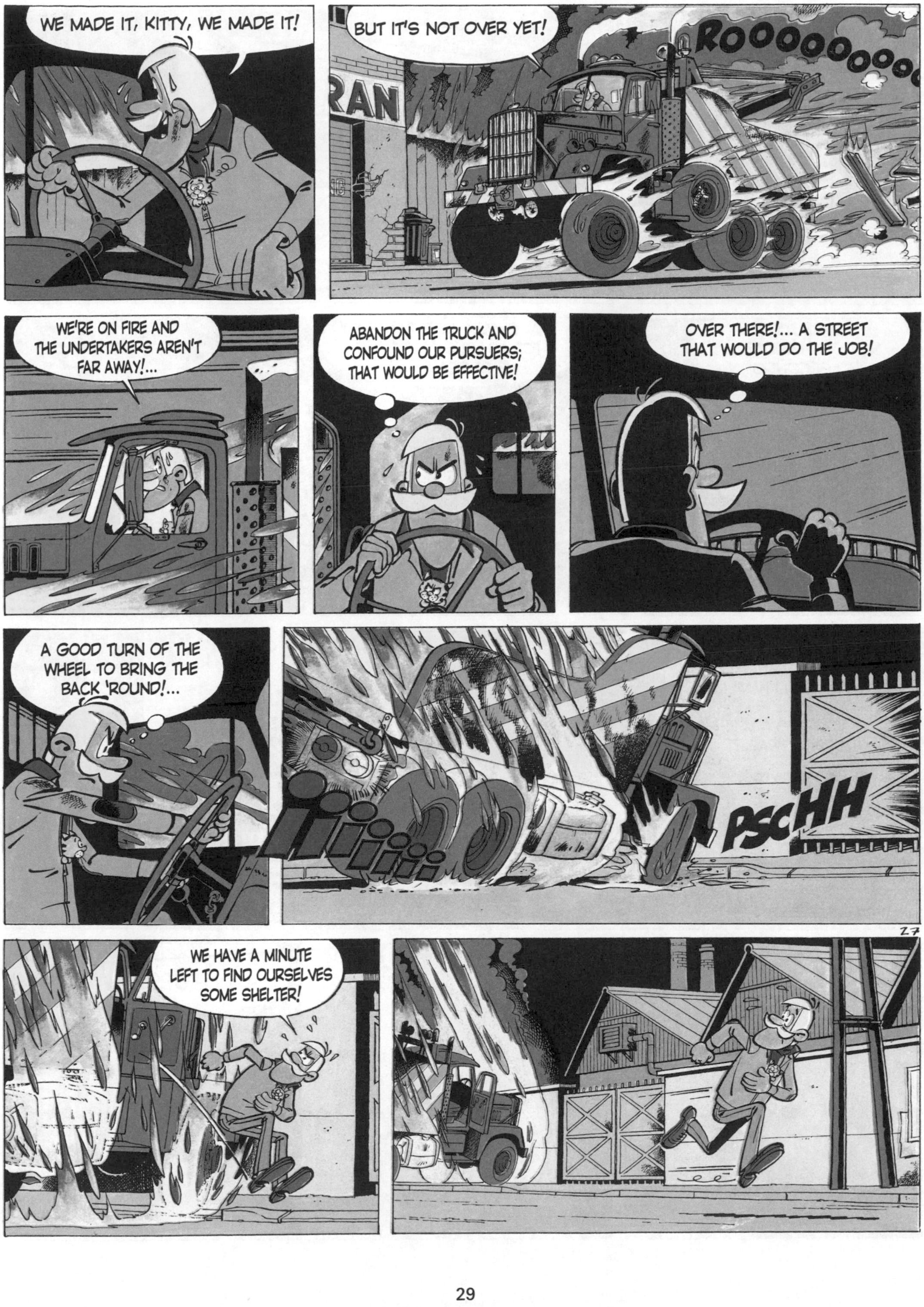
WE MADE IT, KITTY, WE MADE IT!
BUT IT'S NOT OVER YET!
ROOOOOOOOOO
WE'RE ON FIRE AND THE UNDERTAKERS AREN'T FAR AWAY!...
ABANDON THE TRUCK AND CONFOUND OUR PURSUERS; THAT WOULD BE EFFECTIVE!
OVER THERE!... A STREET THAT WOULD DO THE JOB!
A GOOD TURN OF THE WHEEL TO BRING THE BACK 'ROUND!...
iiiiiiiii
PSCHH
WE HAVE A MINUTE LEFT TO FIND OURSELVES SOME SHELTER!

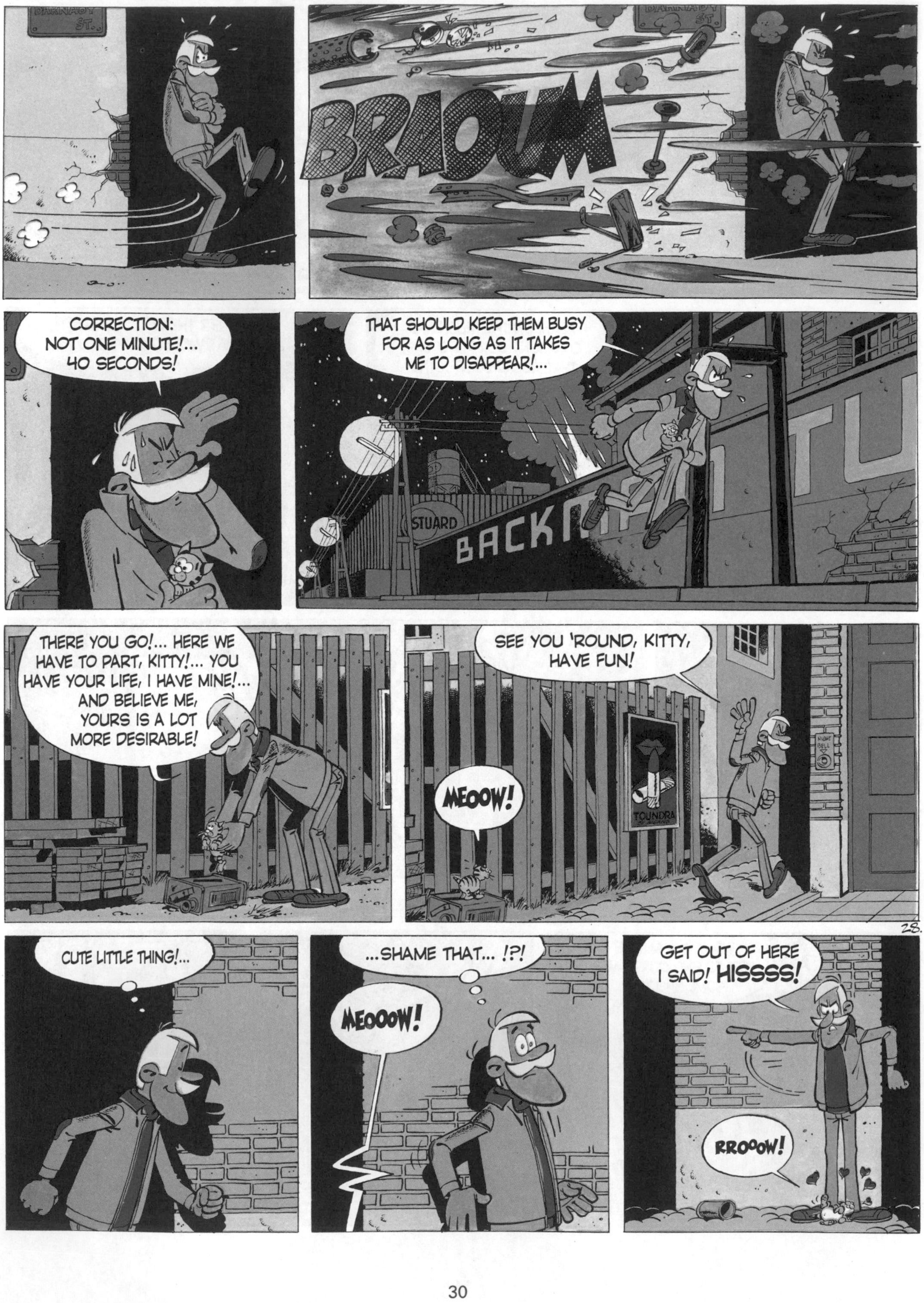
DARNADY ST.
BRAOUM
CORRECTION: NOT ONE MINUTE!... 40 SECONDS!
THAT SHOULD KEEP THEM BUSY FOR AS LONG AS IT TAKES ME TO DISAPPEAR!...
STUARD
BACK
TU
THERE YOU GO!... HERE WE HAVE TO PART, KITTY!... YOU HAVE YOUR LIFE, I HAVE MINE!... AND BELIEVE ME, YOURS IS A LOT MORE DESIRABLE!
SEE YOU 'ROUND, KITTY, HAVE FUN!
MEOOW!
TOUNDRA
NIGHT BELL
28.
CUTE LITTLE THING!...
...SHAME THAT... !?!
MEOOOW!
GET OUT OF HERE I SAID! HISSSS!
RROOOW!

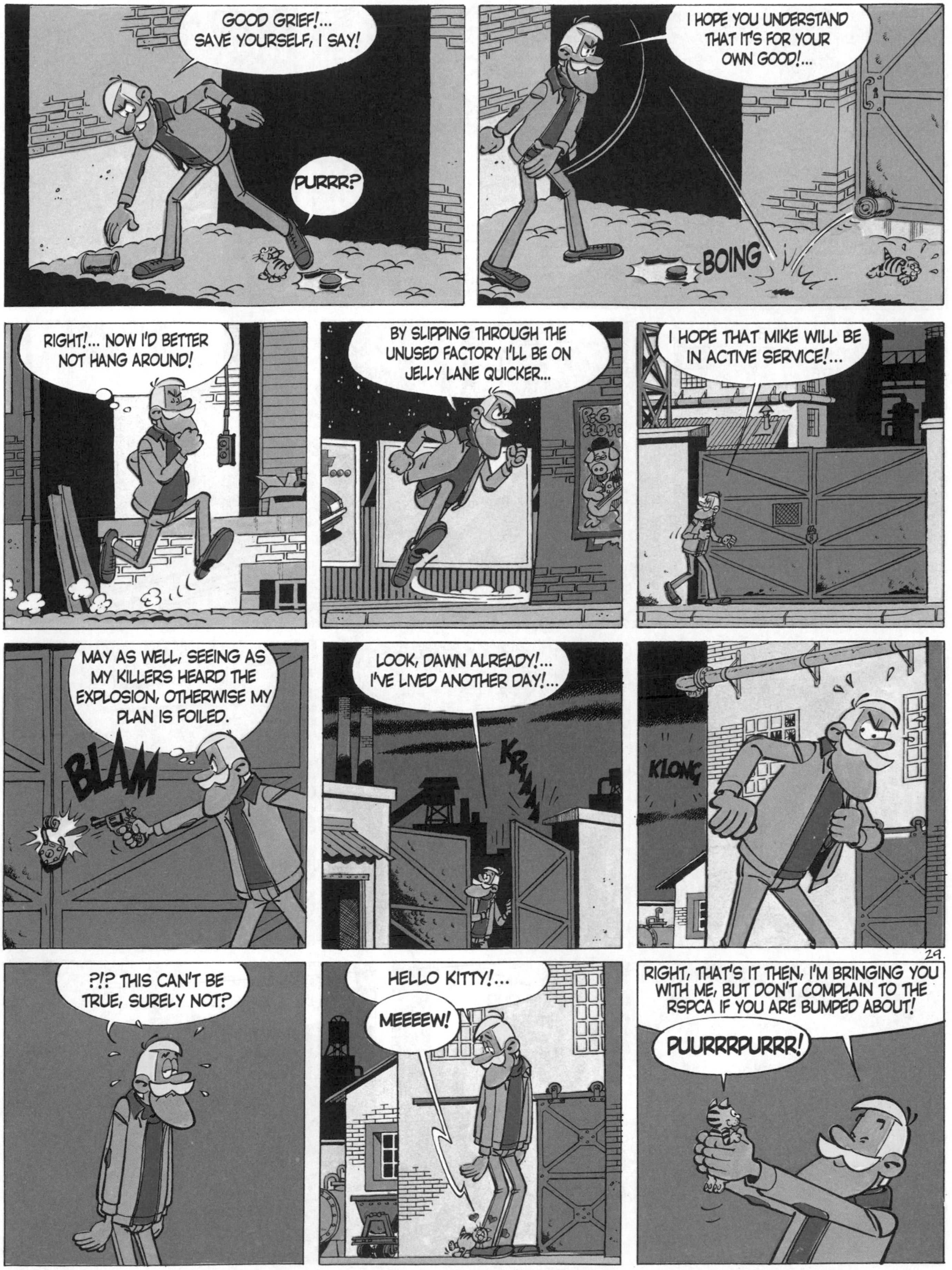
GOOD GRIEF!... SAVE YOURSELF, I SAY!
PURRR?
I HOPE YOU UNDERSTAND THAT IT'S FOR YOUR OWN GOOD!...
BOING
RIGHT!... NOW I'D BETTER NOT HANG AROUND!
BY SLIPPING THROUGH THE UNUSED FACTORY I'LL BE ON JELLY LANE QUICKER...
I HOPE THAT MIKE WILL BE IN ACTIVE SERVICE!...
MAY AS WELL, SEEING AS MY KILLERS HEARD THE EXPLOSION, OTHERWISE MY PLAN IS FOILED.
BLAM
LOOK, DAWN ALREADY!... I'VE LIVED ANOTHER DAY!...
KLONG
?!? THIS CAN'T BE TRUE, SURELY NOT?
HELLO KITTY!...
MEEEEW!
RIGHT, THAT'S IT THEN, I'M BRINGING YOU WITH ME, BUT DON'T COMPLAIN TO THE RSPCA IF YOU ARE BUMPED ABOUT!
PUURRRPURRR!

LET'S GO NOW.
KRIAAA
HOLD ON LITTLE ONE, THERE THEY ARE!
CLOSED, OF COURSE!
CLANG CLANG
JELLY LANE! THIS IS OUR STOP!
THERE! MIKE'S TAXI!... SAVED!...

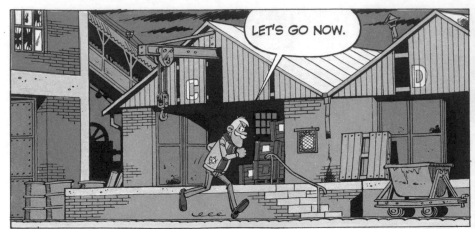

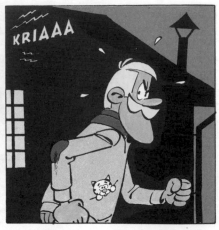

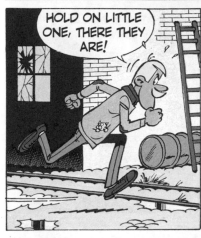

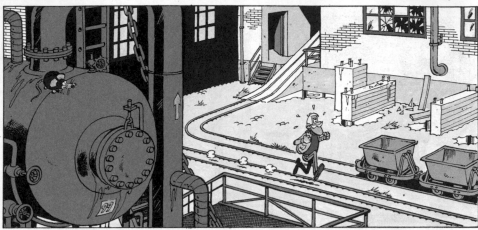

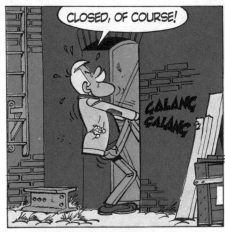

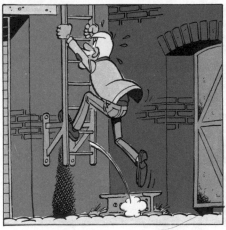

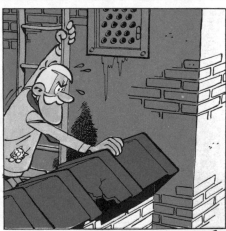

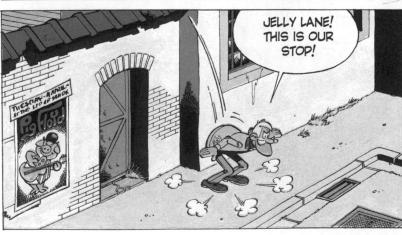

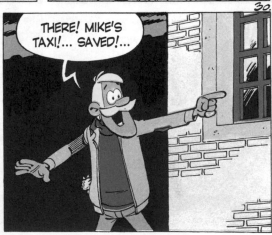

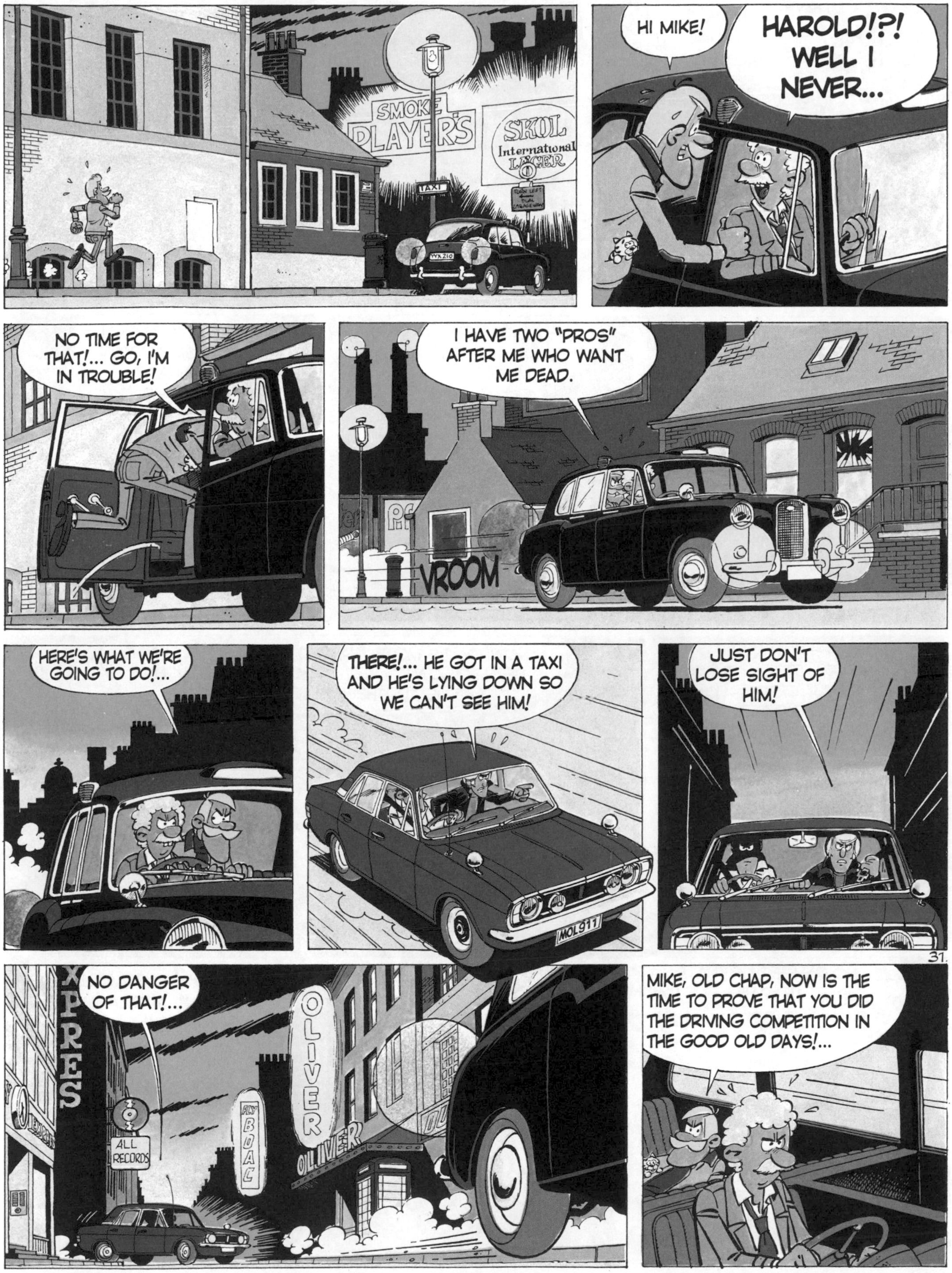
SMOKE PLAYER'S
SKOL International LAGER
TAXI
HI MIKE!
HAROLD!?! WELL I NEVER...
NO TIME FOR THAT!... GO, I'M IN TROUBLE!
I HAVE TWO "PROS" AFTER ME WHO WANT ME DEAD.
VROOM
HERE'S WHAT WE'RE GOING TO DO!...
THERE!... HE GOT IN A TAXI AND HE'S LYING DOWN SO WE CAN'T SEE HIM!
MOL 911
JUST DON'T LOSE SIGHT OF HIM!
31.
XPRES
NO DANGER OF THAT!...
ALL RECORDS
FLY BOAC
OLIVER
MIKE, OLD CHAP, NOW IS THE TIME TO PROVE THAT YOU DID THE DRIVING COMPETITION IN THE GOOD OLD DAYS!...

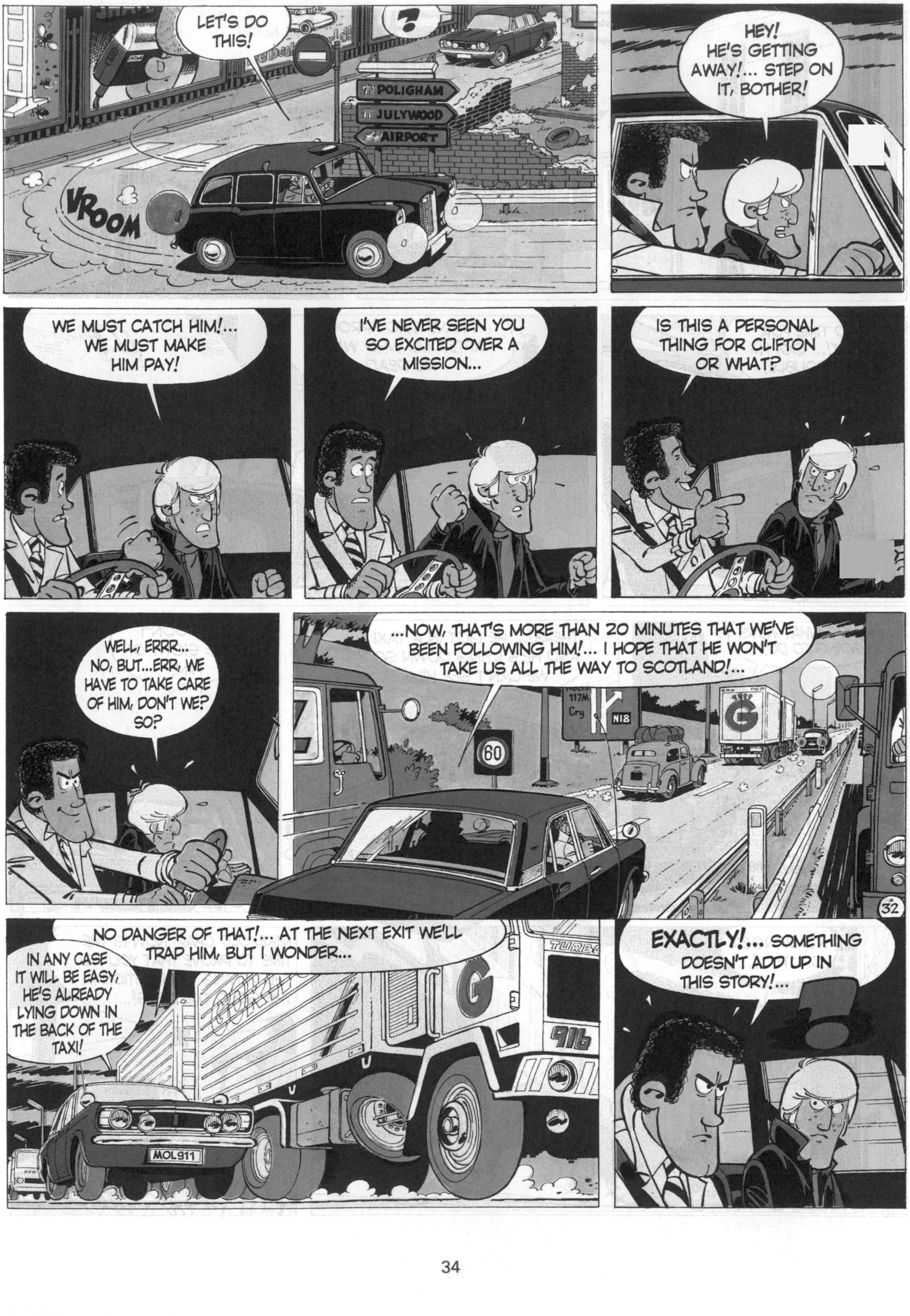
LET'S DO THIS!
?
POLIGHAM
JULYWOOD
AIRPORT
VROOM
HEY! HE'S GETTING AWAY!... STEP ON IT, BOTHER!
WE MUST CATCH HIM!... WE MUST MAKE HIM PAY!
I'VE NEVER SEEN YOU SO EXCITED OVER A MISSION...
IS THIS A PERSONAL THING FOR CLIFTON OR WHAT?
WELL, ERRR... NO, BUT...ERR, WE HAVE TO TAKE CARE OF HIM, DON'T WE? SO?
...NOW, THAT'S MORE THAN 20 MINUTES THAT WE'VE BEEN FOLLOWING HIM!... I HOPE THAT HE WON'T TAKE US ALL THE WAY TO SCOTLAND!...
60
N18
NO DANGER OF THAT!... AT THE NEXT EXIT WE'LL TRAP HIM, BUT I WONDER...
IN ANY CASE IT WILL BE EASY, HE'S ALREADY LYING DOWN IN THE BACK OF THE TAXI!
MOL 911
EXACTLY!... SOMETHING DOESN'T ADD UP IN THIS STORY!...

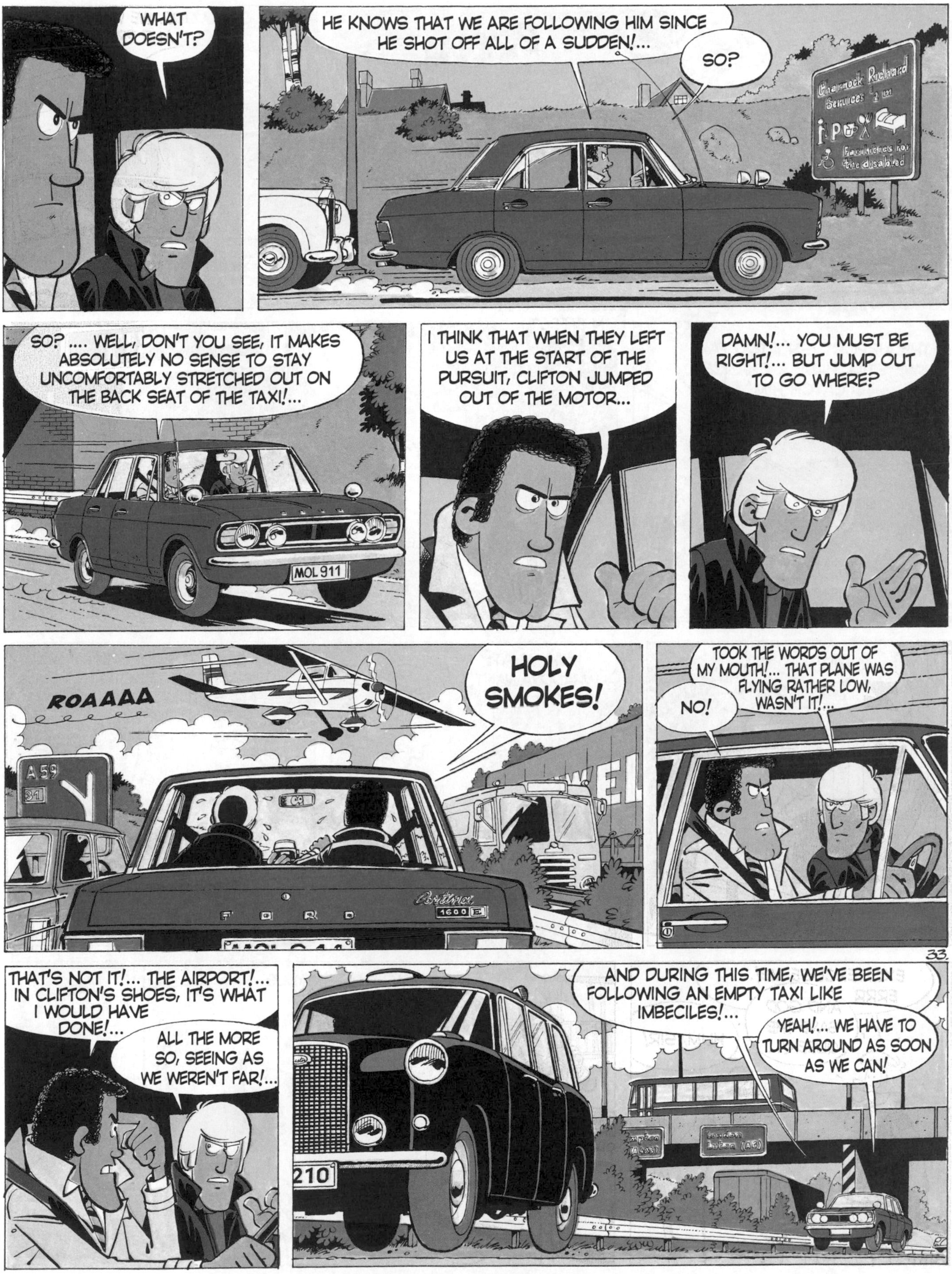
WHAT DOESN'T?
HE KNOWS THAT WE ARE FOLLOWING HIM SINCE HE SHOT OFF ALL OF A SUDDEN!...
SO?
Charnock Richard Services ½ m
Facilities for the disabled
SO? .... WELL, DON'T YOU SEE, IT MAKES ABSOLUTELY NO SENSE TO STAY UNCOMFORTABLY STRETCHED OUT ON THE BACK SEAT OF THE TAXI!...
MOL 911
I THINK THAT WHEN THEY LEFT US AT THE START OF THE PURSUIT, CLIFTON JUMPED OUT OF THE MOTOR...
DAMN!... YOU MUST BE RIGHT!... BUT JUMP OUT TO GO WHERE?
ROAAAA
HOLY SMOKES!
A 59
31
FORD
Cortina 1600 E
TOOK THE WORDS OUT OF MY MOUTH!... THAT PLANE WAS FLYING RATHER LOW, WASN'T IT!...
NO!
THAT'S NOT IT!... THE AIRPORT!... IN CLIFTON'S SHOES, IT'S WHAT I WOULD HAVE DONE!...
ALL THE MORE SO, SEEING AS WE WEREN'T FAR!...
AND DURING THIS TIME, WE'VE BEEN FOLLOWING AN EMPTY TAXI LIKE IMBECILES!...
YEAH!... WE HAVE TO TURN AROUND AS SOON AS WE CAN!
210

TUUUT
PWAAAA
LENON & MCARTNEY
MOL911
VROOM
IIIIAA
GOOD GOD, WE WERE HAD GOOD AND PROPER!
NOT FOR LONG!
VROOOOOOOO
THE AIRPORT ISN'T TOO FAR, WE STILL HAVE A CHANCE TO CATCH HIM!
London Luton (A6)
ROOOO
IN EFFECT...
EXIT
BEA
08 22
FLY AIR ZATZ
Z
SIR!
Z
HUH, WHAT? WHADDYAWANT?
YOU CAN'T SLEEP THERE!... THIS ATTITUDE IS NOT AT ALL BEFITTING OF A BRITISH SUBJECT!...
EXC...EXCUSE ME!... ERRR
AND GOD SAVE THE QUEEN!...
HUM, SIR!
...I'M DEAD WITH FATIGUE AND OWW... THAT HUMMING!

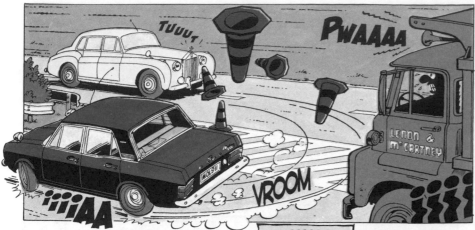

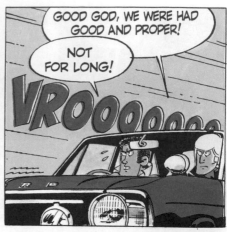

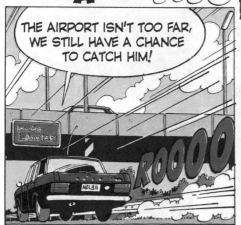

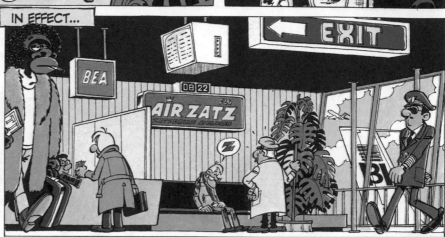

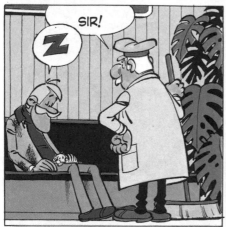

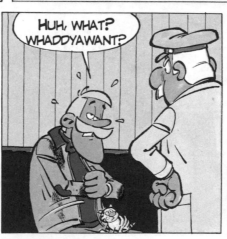

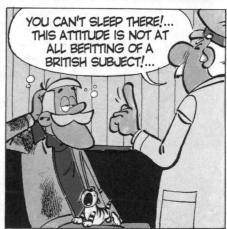

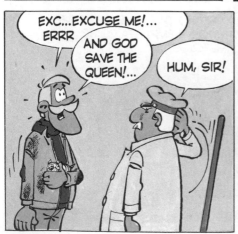

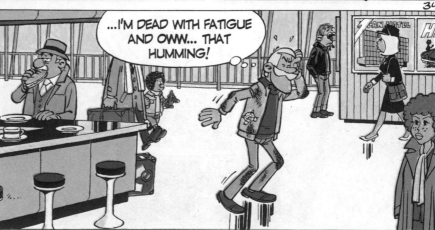

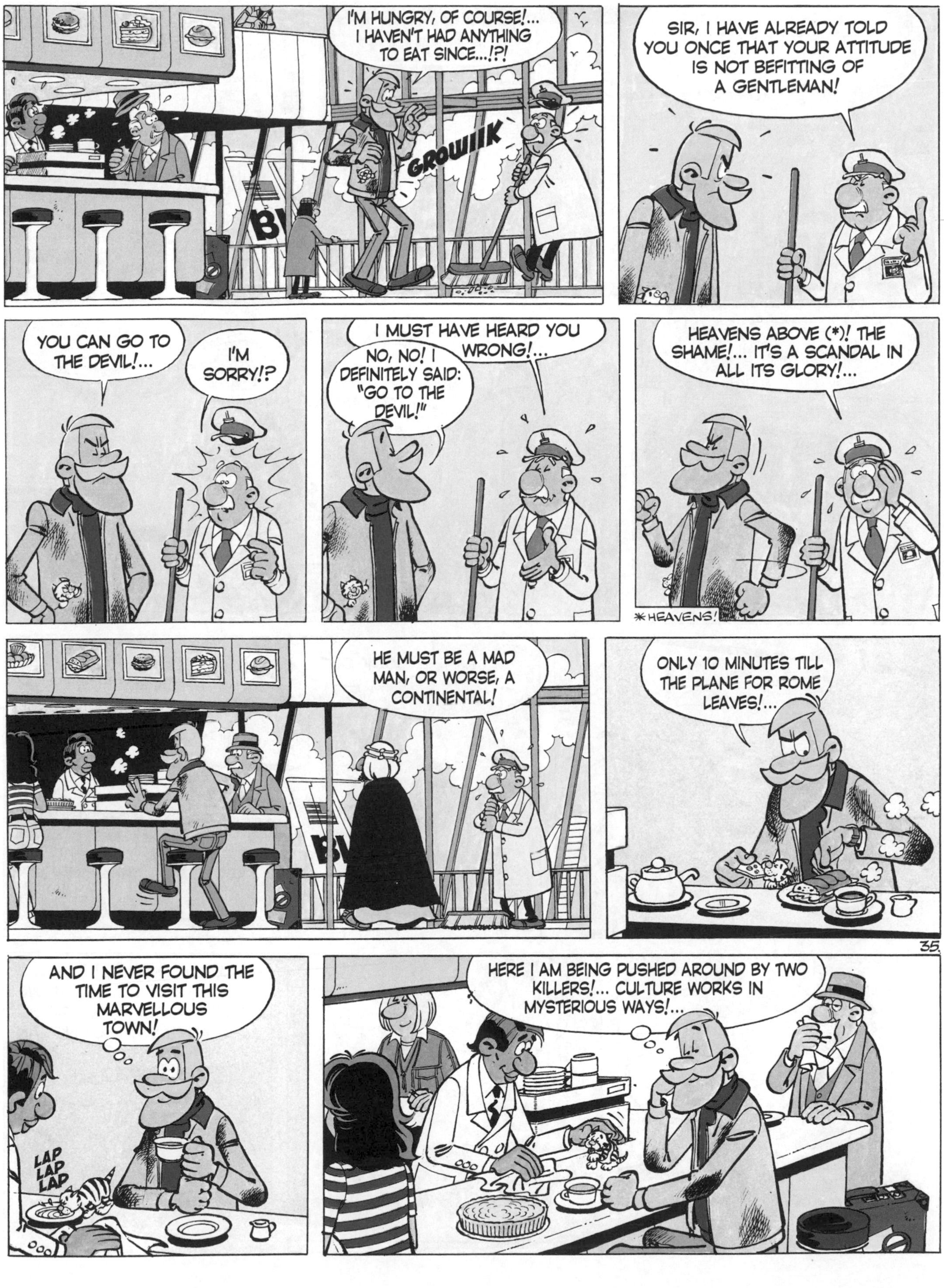
I'M HUNGRY, OF COURSE!... I HAVEN'T HAD ANYTHING TO EAT SINCE...!?!
GROWIIIK
SIR, I HAVE ALREADY TOLD YOU ONCE THAT YOUR ATTITUDE IS NOT BEFITTING OF A GENTLEMAN!
YOU CAN GO TO THE DEVIL!...
I'M SORRY!?
I MUST HAVE HEARD YOU WRONG!...
NO, NO! I DEFINITELY SAID: "GO TO THE DEVIL!"
HEAVENS ABOVE (*)! THE SHAME!... IT'S A SCANDAL IN ALL ITS GLORY!...
* HEAVENS!
HE MUST BE A MAD MAN, OR WORSE, A CONTINENTAL!
ONLY 10 MINUTES TILL THE PLANE FOR ROME LEAVES!...
35
AND I NEVER FOUND THE TIME TO VISIT THIS MARVELLOUS TOWN!
LAP LAP LAP
HERE I AM BEING PUSHED AROUND BY TWO KILLERS!... CULTURE WORKS IN MYSTERIOUS WAYS!...

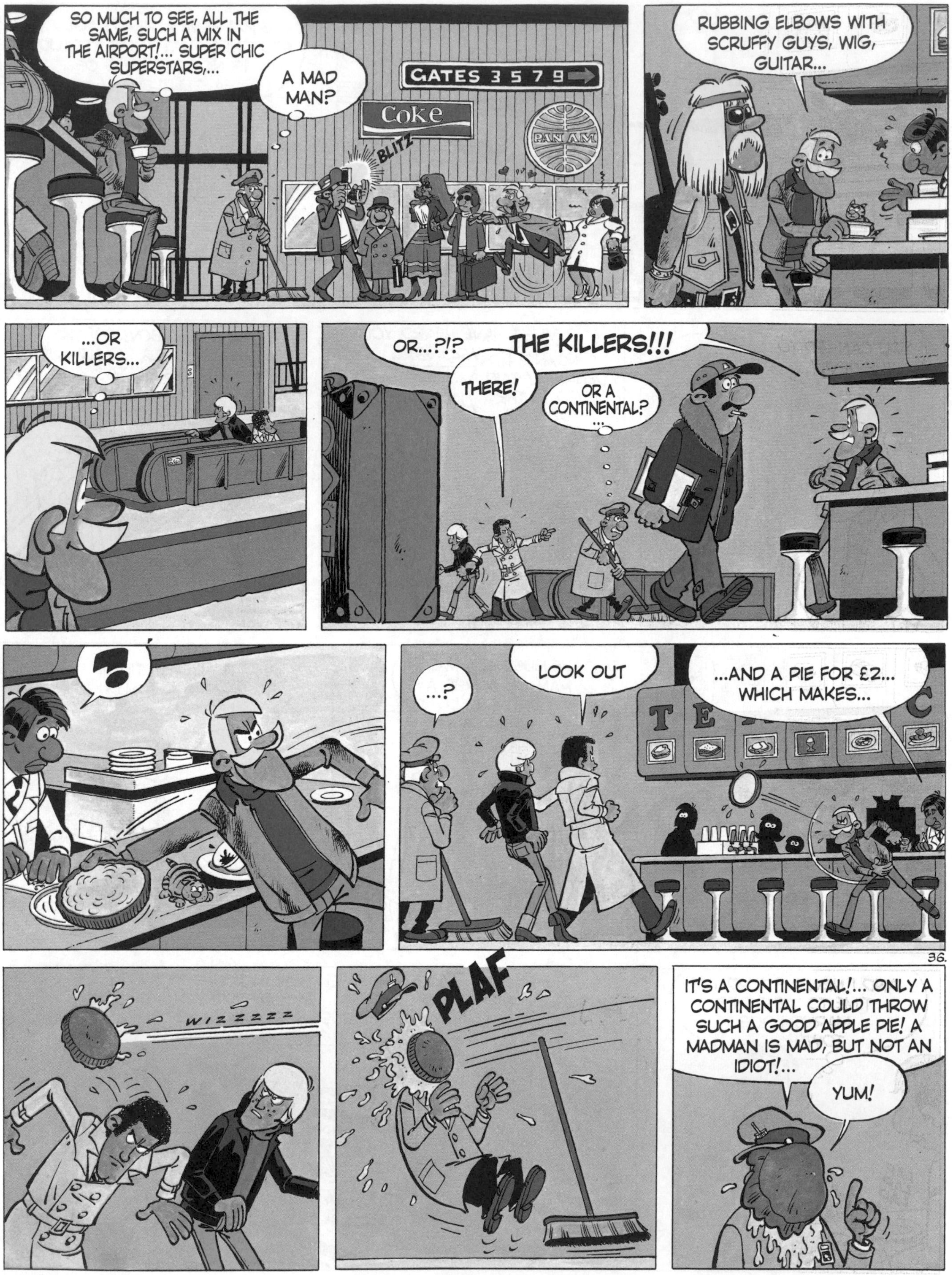
SO MUCH TO SEE, ALL THE SAME, SUCH A MIX IN THE AIRPORT!... SUPER CHIC SUPERSTARS,...
A MAD MAN?
GATES 3 5 7 9
Coke
PAN AM
BLITZ
RUBBING ELBOWS WITH SCRUFFY GUYS, WIG, GUITAR...
...OR KILLERS...
OR...?!?
THE KILLERS!!!
THERE!
OR A CONTINENTAL? ...
...?
LOOK OUT
...AND A PIE FOR £2... WHICH MAKES...
36.
WIZZZZZ
PLAF
IT'S A CONTINENTAL!... ONLY A CONTINENTAL COULD THROW SUCH A GOOD APPLE PIE! A MADMAN IS MAD, BUT NOT AN IDIOT!...
YUM!

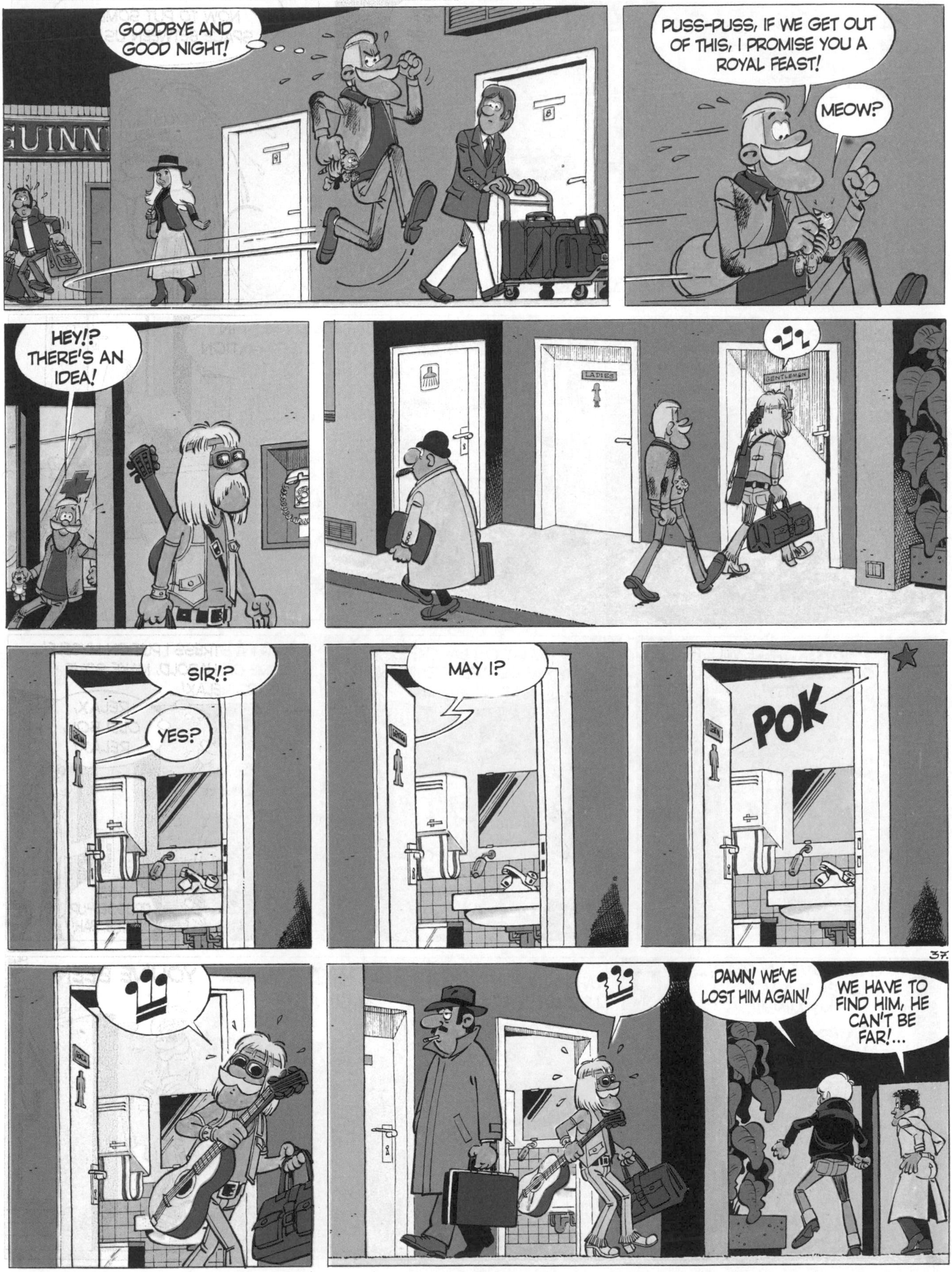
GOODBYE AND GOOD NIGHT!
GUINN
PUSS-PUSS, IF WE GET OUT OF THIS, I PROMISE YOU A ROYAL FEAST!
MEOW?
HEY!? THERE'S AN IDEA!
LADIES
GENTLEMEN
SIR!?
YES?
MAY I?
POK
37.
DAMN! WE'VE LOST HIM AGAIN!
WE HAVE TO FIND HIM, HE CAN'T BE FAR!...

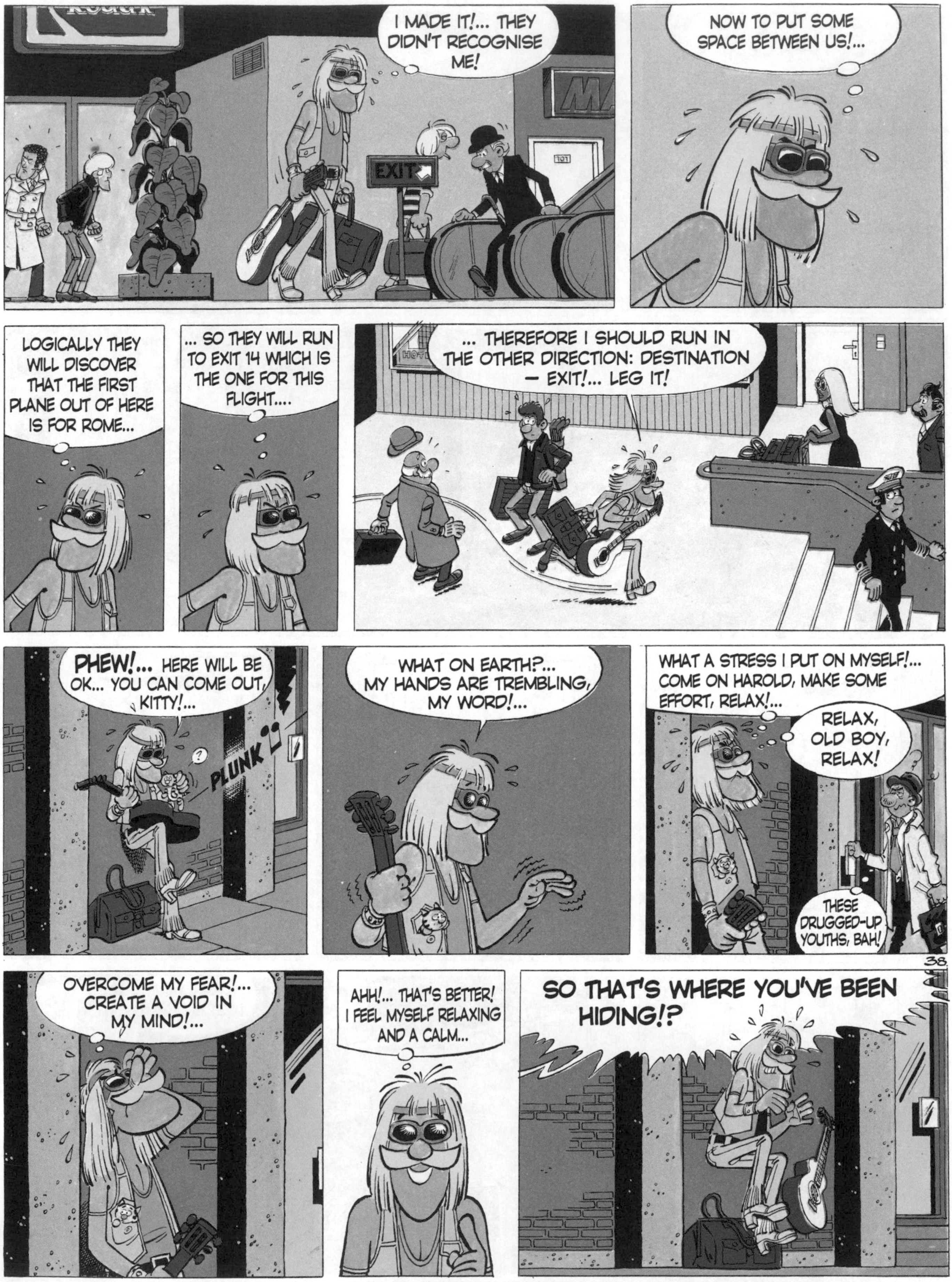

I MADE IT!... THEY DIDN'T RECOGNISE ME!
EXIT
NOW TO PUT SOME SPACE BETWEEN US!...
LOGICALLY THEY WILL DISCOVER THAT THE FIRST PLANE OUT OF HERE IS FOR ROME...
... SO THEY WILL RUN TO EXIT 14 WHICH IS THE ONE FOR THIS FLIGHT....
... THEREFORE I SHOULD RUN IN THE OTHER DIRECTION: DESTINATION — EXIT!... LEG IT!
PHEW!... HERE WILL BE OK... YOU CAN COME OUT, KITTY!...
?
PLUNK
WHAT ON EARTH?... MY HANDS ARE TREMBLING, MY WORD!...
WHAT A STRESS I PUT ON MYSELF!... COME ON HAROLD, MAKE SOME EFFORT, RELAX!...
RELAX, OLD BOY, RELAX!
THESE DRUGGED-UP YOUTHS, BAH!
OVERCOME MY FEAR!... CREATE A VOID IN MY MIND!...
AHH!... THAT'S BETTER! I FEEL MYSELF RELAXING AND A CALM...
SO THAT'S WHERE YOU'VE BEEN HIDING!?

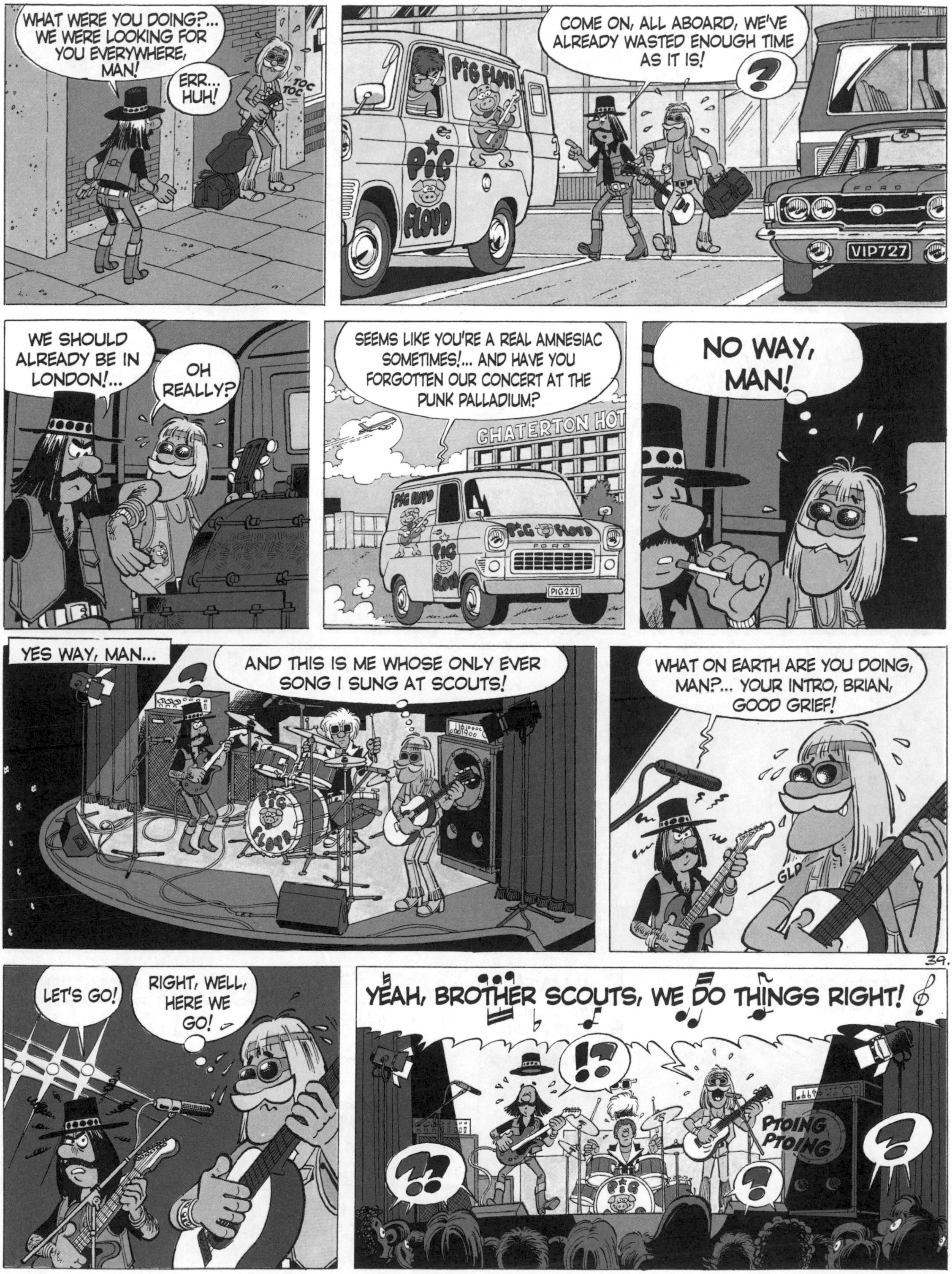
WHAT WERE YOU DOING?... WE WERE LOOKING FOR YOU EVERYWHERE, MAN!
ERR... HUH!
TOC TOC
COME ON, ALL ABOARD, WE'VE ALREADY WASTED ENOUGH TIME AS IT IS!
?
PIG FLOYD
FORD
VIP727
WE SHOULD ALREADY BE IN LONDON!...
OH REALLY?
SEEMS LIKE YOU'RE A REAL AMNESIAC SOMETIMES!... AND HAVE YOU FORGOTTEN OUR CONCERT AT THE PUNK PALLADIUM?
CHATERTON HOT
PIG221
NO WAY, MAN!
YES WAY, MAN...
AND THIS IS ME WHOSE ONLY EVER SONG I SUNG AT SCOUTS!
WHAT ON EARTH ARE YOU DOING, MAN?... YOUR INTRO, BRIAN, GOOD GRIEF!
GLP
34.
LET'S GO!
RIGHT, WELL, HERE WE GO!
YEAH, BROTHER SCOUTS, WE DO THINGS RIGHT!
!?
PTOING PTOING
?

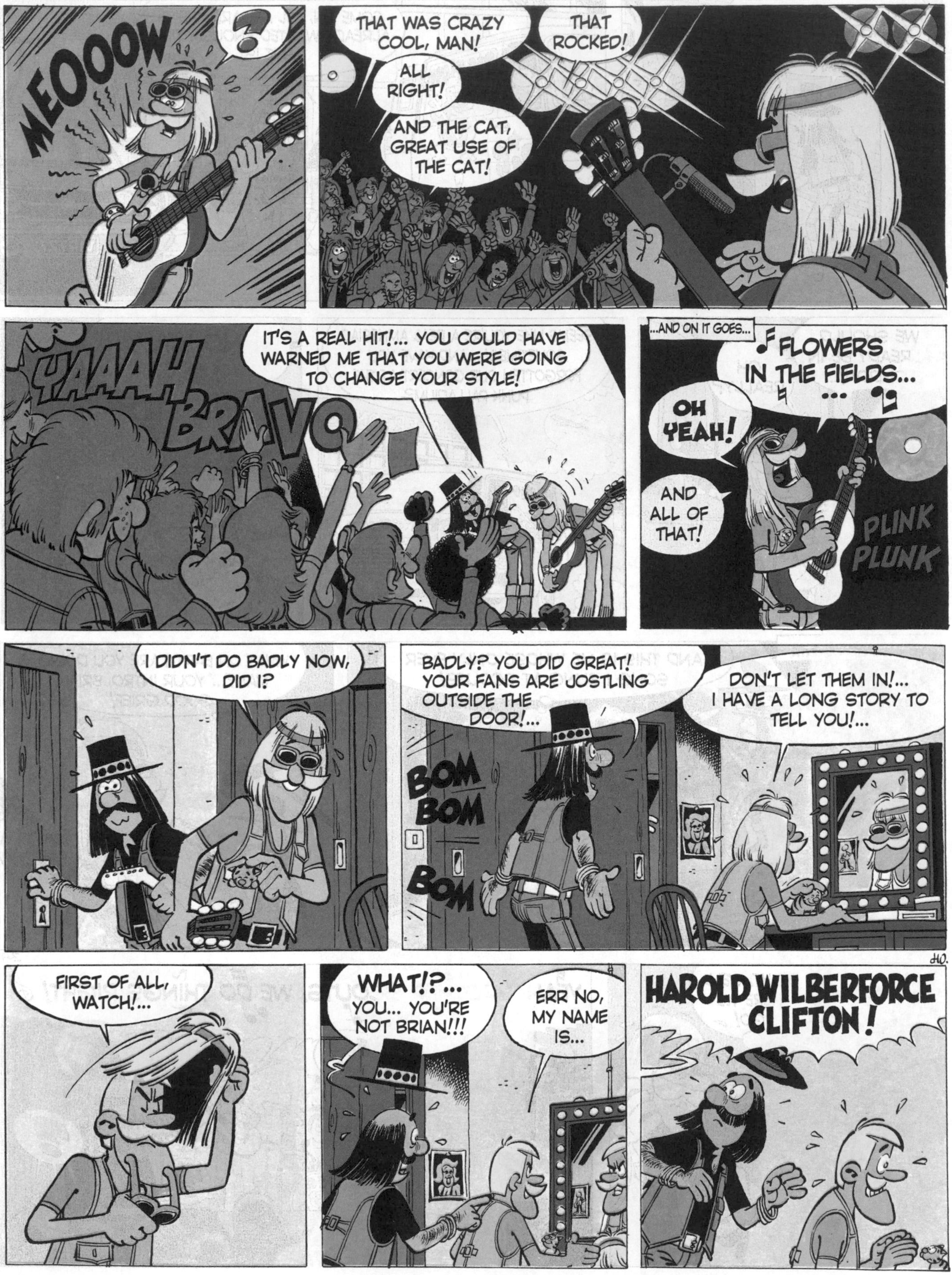

MEOOOW
?
THAT WAS CRAZY COOL, MAN!
THAT ROCKED!
ALL RIGHT!
AND THE CAT, GREAT USE OF THE CAT!
YAAAH BRAVO
IT'S A REAL HIT!... YOU COULD HAVE WARNED ME THAT YOU WERE GOING TO CHANGE YOUR STYLE!
...AND ON IT GOES...
FLOWERS IN THE FIELDS... ...
OH YEAH!
AND ALL OF THAT!
PLINK PLUNK
I DIDN'T DO BADLY NOW, DID I?
BADLY? YOU DID GREAT! YOUR FANS ARE JOSTLING OUTSIDE THE DOOR!...
DON'T LET THEM IN!... I HAVE A LONG STORY TO TELL YOU!...
BOM BOM BOM
FIRST OF ALL, WATCH!...
WHAT!?... YOU... YOU'RE NOT BRIAN!!!
ERR NO, MY NAME IS...
HAROLD WILBERFORCE CLIFTON!

CHAPS, IF IT'S FOR AN AUTOGRAPH...
YES, THAT'S EXACTLY WHY WE ARE HERE!
LOOK HERE, I EVEN HAVE MY PEN!...
BUT WHAT THE...!?
KLAK
SILENCE OR I'LL CUT YOUR WORDS SHORT!
...WHEN WE FOUND THE GUY IN HIS UNDERPANTS IN THE TOILETS, IT DIDN'T TAKE US LONG!...
BOM
HEY, LADS, THE PUBLIC ARE CALLING FOR YOU!...
PAF
SHHH
TAK
HA!
THAT'S SOME REAL HARD ROCK!

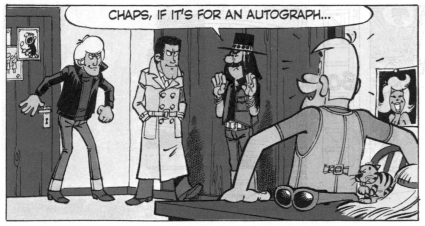

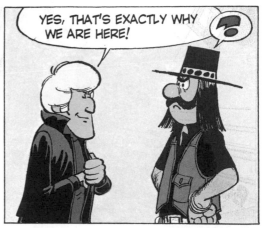

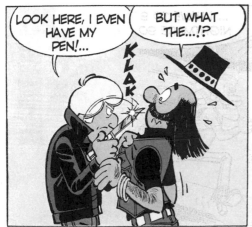

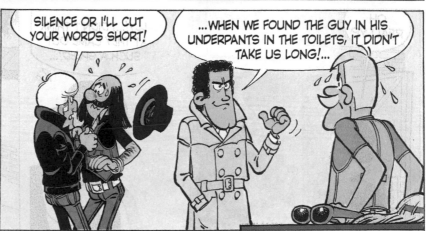

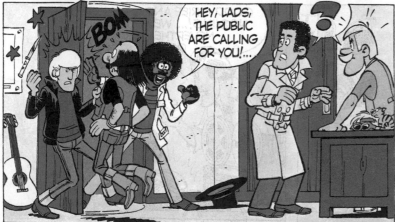

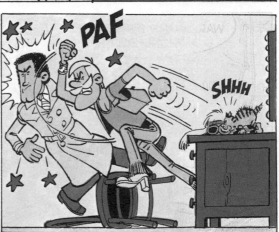

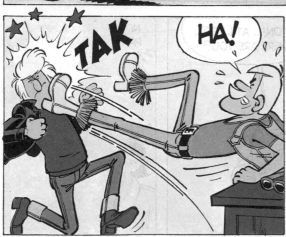

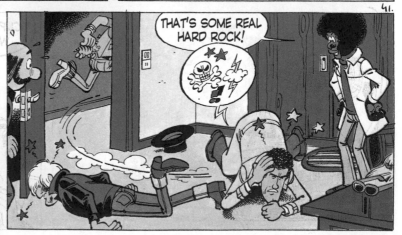

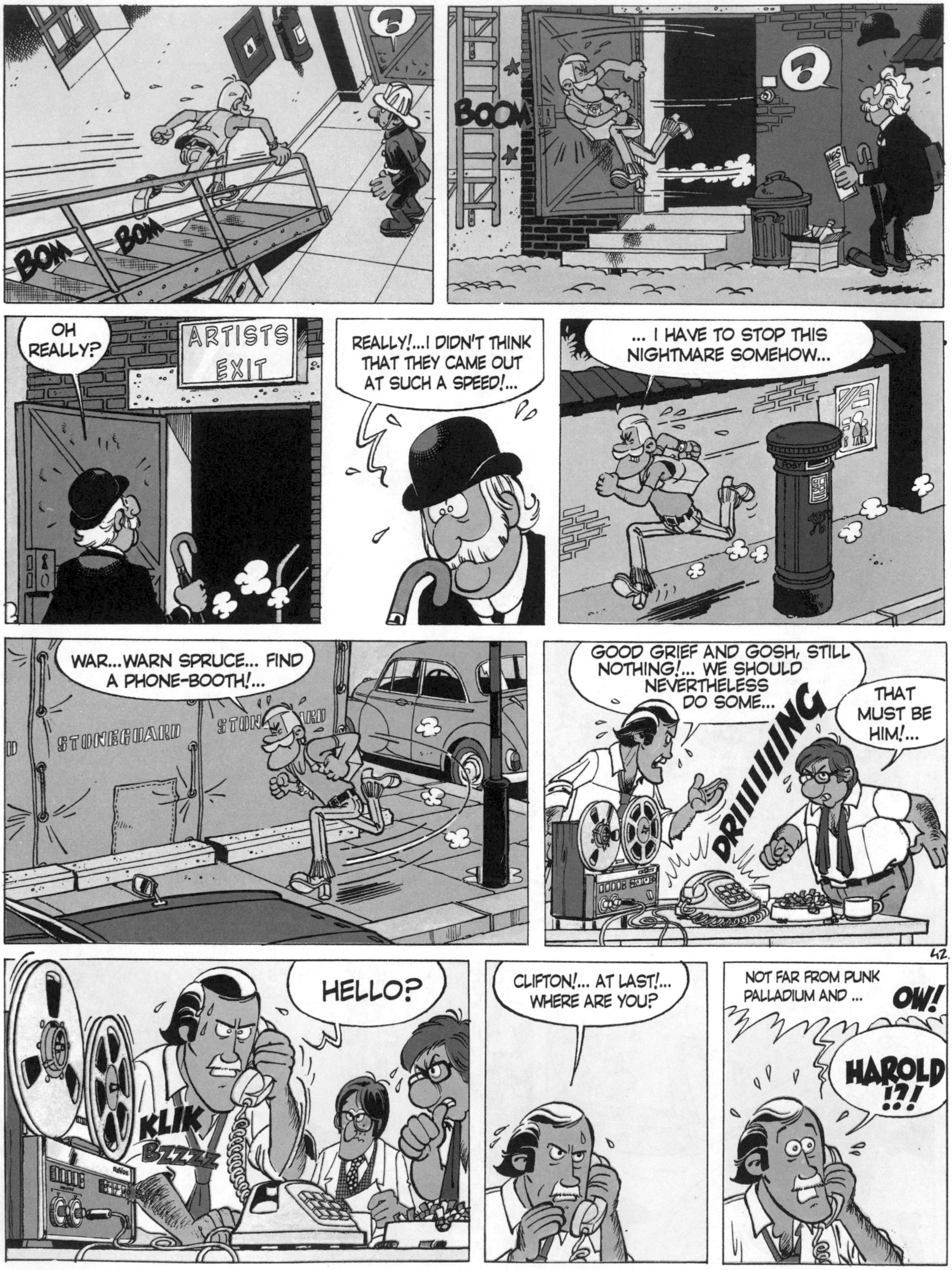
BOM
BOM
?
BOOM
?
OH REALLY?
ARTISTS EXIT
REALLY!... I DIDN'T THINK THAT THEY CAME OUT AT SUCH A SPEED!...
... I HAVE TO STOP THIS NIGHTMARE SOMEHOW...
WAR... WARN SPRUCE... FIND A PHONE-BOOTH!...
STONEGUARD
GOOD GRIEF AND GOSH, STILL NOTHING!... WE SHOULD NEVERTHELESS DO SOME...
DRIIIIIIING
THAT MUST BE HIM!...
HELLO?
KLIK
BZZZZ
CLIFTON!... AT LAST!... WHERE ARE YOU?
NOT FAR FROM PUNK PALLADIUM AND ...
OW!
HAROLD !?!

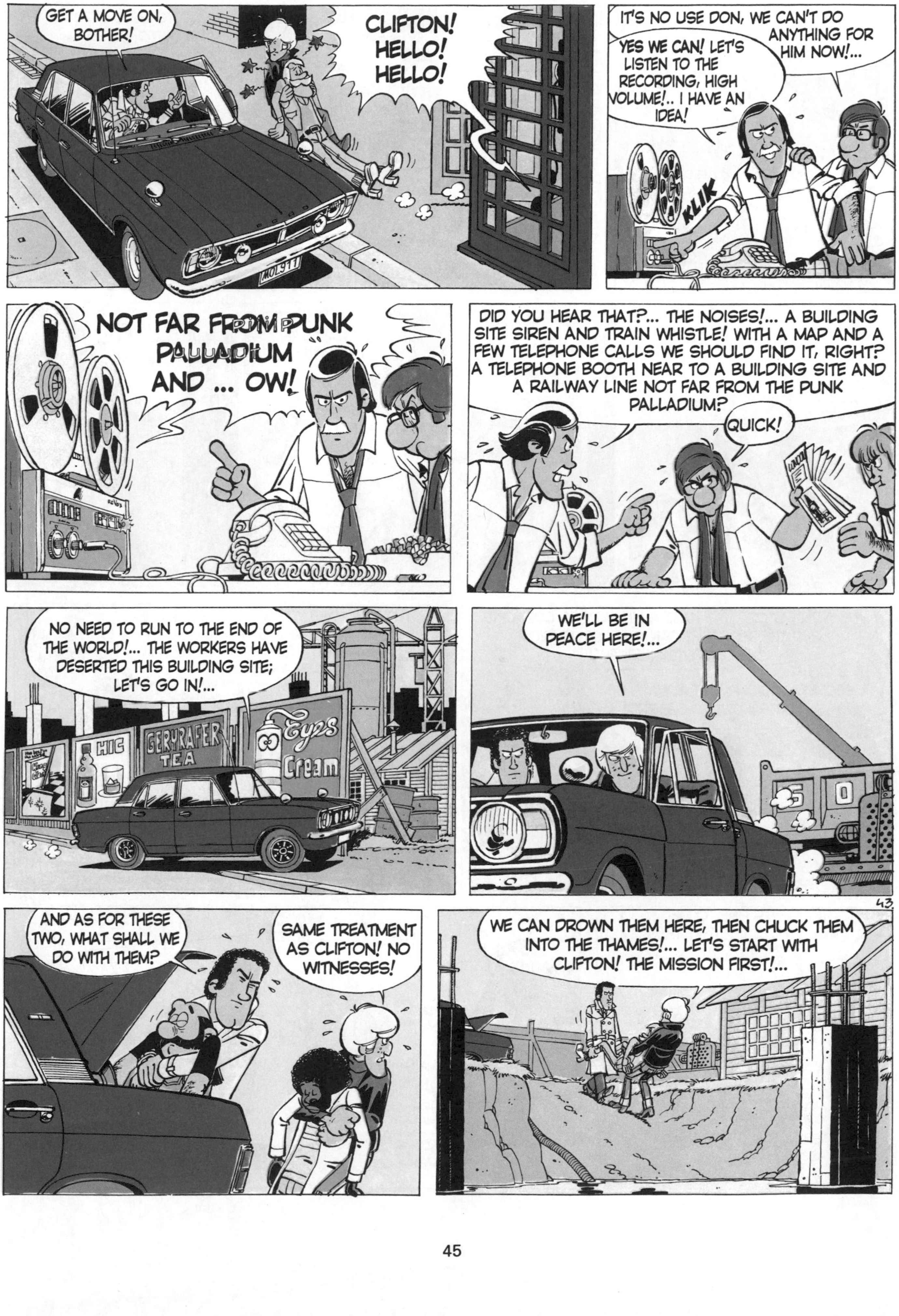
GET A MOVE ON, BOTHER!
CLIFTON! HELLO! HELLO!
IT'S NO USE DON, WE CAN'T DO ANYTHING FOR HIM NOW!...
YES WE CAN! LET'S LISTEN TO THE RECORDING, HIGH VOLUME!.. I HAVE AN IDEA!
KLIK
NOT FAR FROM PUNK PALLADIUM AND ... OW!
DID YOU HEAR THAT?... THE NOISES!... A BUILDING SITE SIREN AND TRAIN WHISTLE! WITH A MAP AND A FEW TELEPHONE CALLS WE SHOULD FIND IT, RIGHT? A TELEPHONE BOOTH NEAR TO A BUILDING SITE AND A RAILWAY LINE NOT FAR FROM THE PUNK PALLADIUM?
QUICK!
NO NEED TO RUN TO THE END OF THE WORLD!... THE WORKERS HAVE DESERTED THIS BUILDING SITE; LET'S GO IN!...
HIC
GERYRAFER TEA
Eyes Cream
WE'LL BE IN PEACE HERE!...
43
AND AS FOR THESE TWO, WHAT SHALL WE DO WITH THEM?
SAME TREATMENT AS CLIFTON! NO WITNESSES!
WE CAN DROWN THEM HERE, THEN CHUCK THEM INTO THE THAMES!... LET'S START WITH CLIFTON! THE MISSION FIRST!...

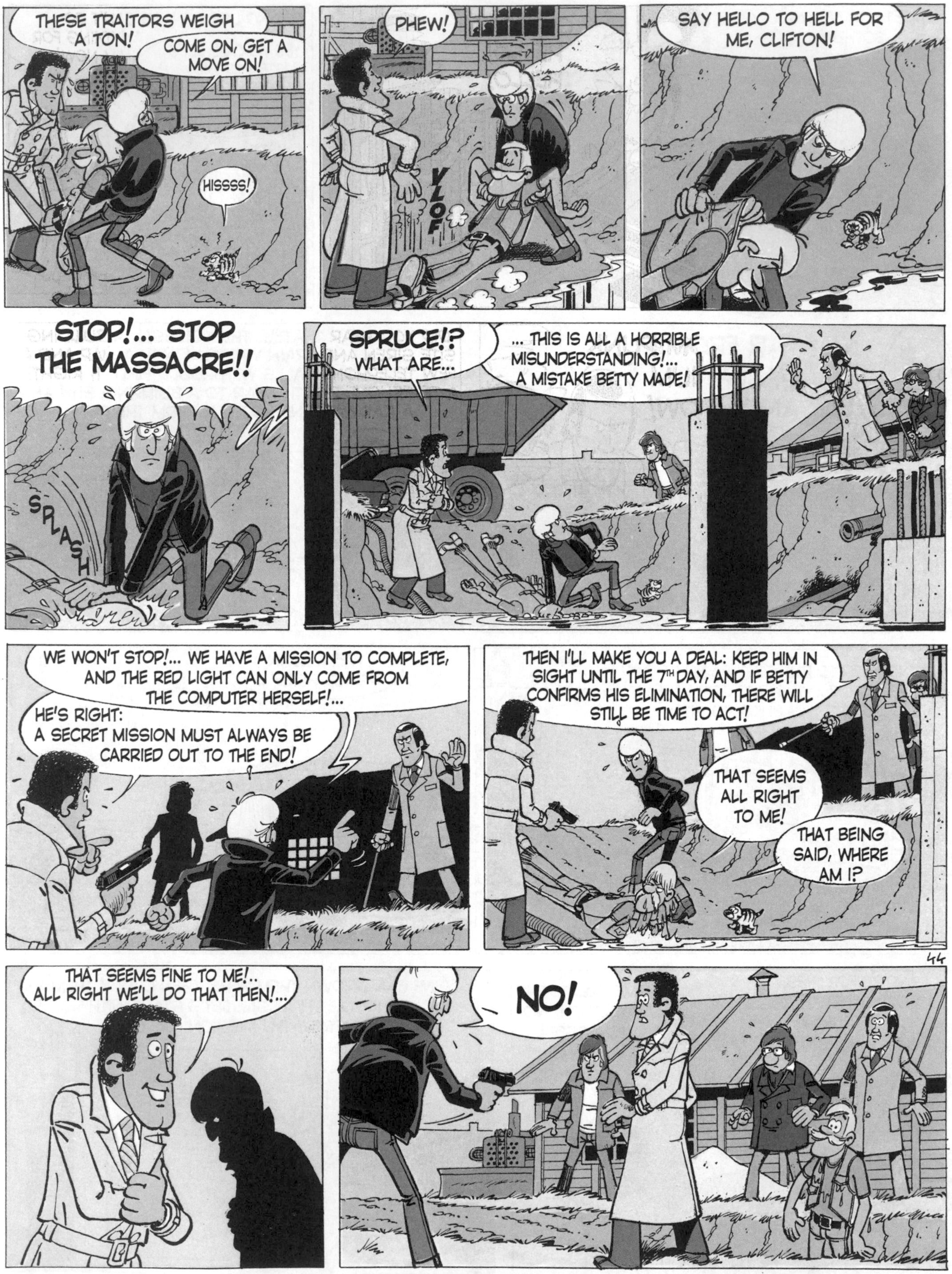
THESE TRAITORS WEIGH A TON!
COME ON, GET A MOVE ON!
HISSSS!
PHEW!
VLOOF
SAY HELLO TO HELL FOR ME, CLIFTON!
STOP!... STOP THE MASSACRE!!
SPLASH
SPRUCE!? WHAT ARE...
... THIS IS ALL A HORRIBLE MISUNDERSTANDING!... A MISTAKE BETTY MADE!
WE WON'T STOP!... WE HAVE A MISSION TO COMPLETE, AND THE RED LIGHT CAN ONLY COME FROM THE COMPUTER HERSELF!...
HE'S RIGHT: A SECRET MISSION MUST ALWAYS BE CARRIED OUT TO THE END!
THEN I'LL MAKE YOU A DEAL: KEEP HIM IN SIGHT UNTIL THE 7TH DAY, AND IF BETTY CONFIRMS HIS ELIMINATION, THERE WILL STILL BE TIME TO ACT!
THAT SEEMS ALL RIGHT TO ME!
THAT BEING SAID, WHERE AM I?
44
THAT SEEMS FINE TO ME!.. ALL RIGHT WE'LL DO THAT THEN!...
NO!

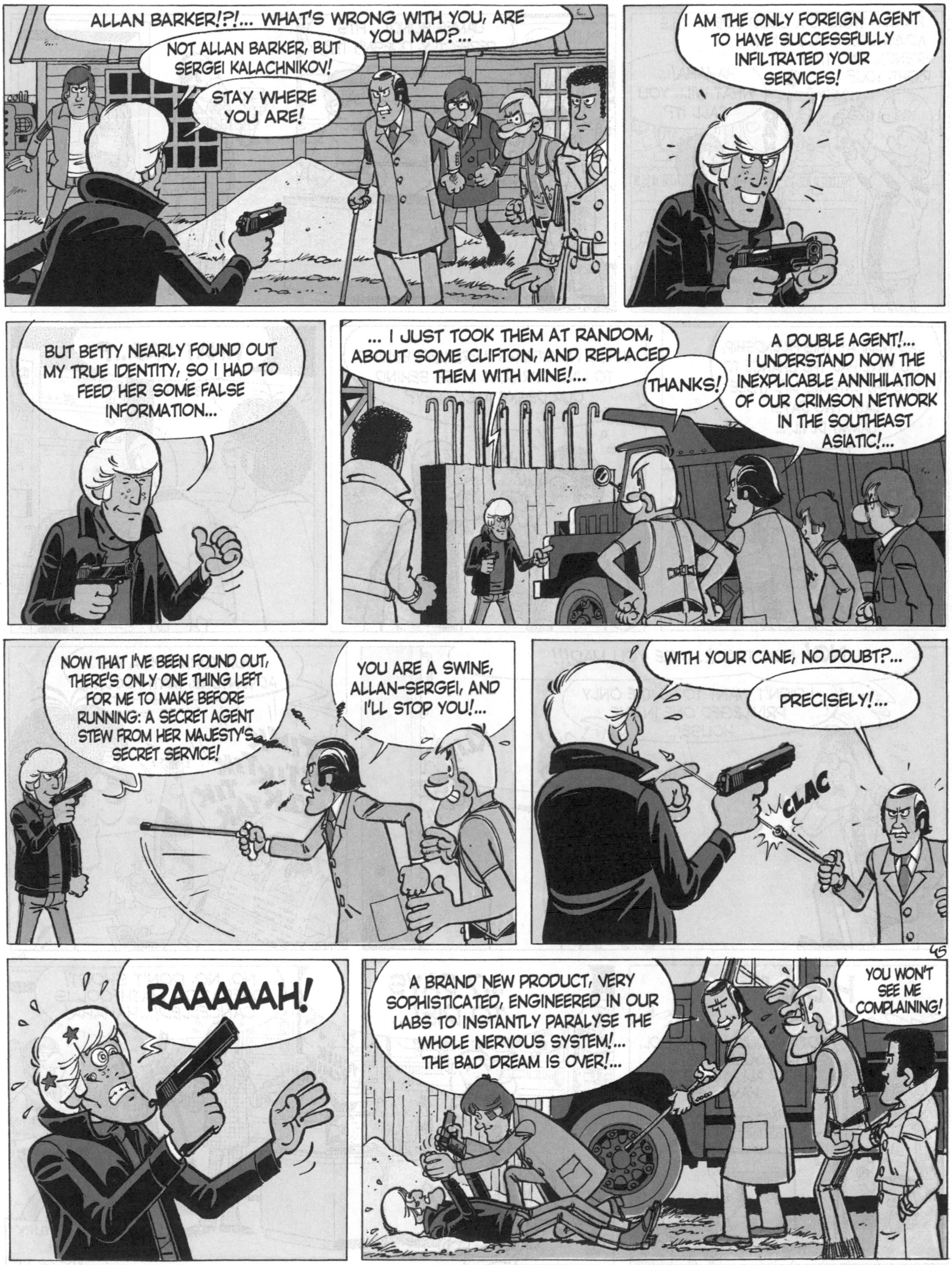
ALLAN BARKER!?!... WHAT'S WRONG WITH YOU, ARE YOU MAD?...
NOT ALLAN BARKER, BUT SERGEI KALACHNIKOV!
STAY WHERE YOU ARE!
I AM THE ONLY FOREIGN AGENT TO HAVE SUCCESSFULLY INFILTRATED YOUR SERVICES!
BUT BETTY NEARLY FOUND OUT MY TRUE IDENTITY, SO I HAD TO FEED HER SOME FALSE INFORMATION...
... I JUST TOOK THEM AT RANDOM, ABOUT SOME CLIFTON, AND REPLACED THEM WITH MINE!...
THANKS!
A DOUBLE AGENT!... I UNDERSTAND NOW THE INEXPLICABLE ANNIHILATION OF OUR CRIMSON NETWORK IN THE SOUTHEAST ASIATIC!...
NOW THAT I'VE BEEN FOUND OUT, THERE'S ONLY ONE THING LEFT FOR ME TO MAKE BEFORE RUNNING: A SECRET AGENT STEW FROM HER MAJESTY'S SECRET SERVICE!
YOU ARE A SWINE, ALLAN-SERGEI, AND I'LL STOP YOU!...
WITH YOUR CANE, NO DOUBT?...
PRECISELY!...
CLAC
RAAAAAH!
A BRAND NEW PRODUCT, VERY SOPHISTICATED, ENGINEERED IN OUR LABS TO INSTANTLY PARALYSE THE WHOLE NERVOUS SYSTEM!... THE BAD DREAM IS OVER!...
YOU WON'T SEE ME COMPLAINING!

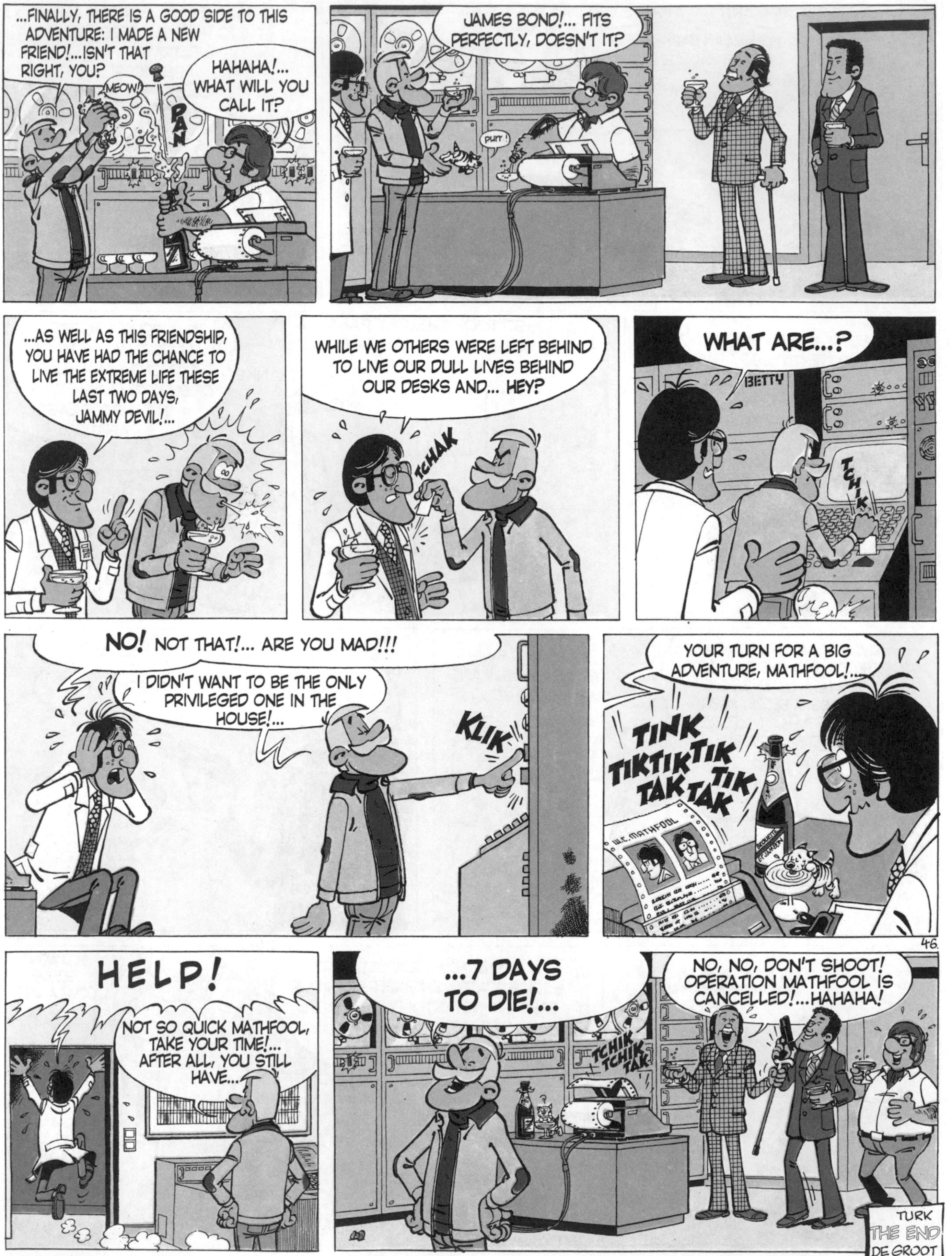
...FINALLY, THERE IS A GOOD SIDE TO THIS ADVENTURE: I MADE A NEW FRIEND!...ISN'T THAT RIGHT, YOU?
MEOW!
PAN
HAHAHA!... WHAT WILL YOU CALL IT?
JAMES BOND!... FITS PERFECTLY, DOESN'T IT?
PUIT!
...AS WELL AS THIS FRIENDSHIP, YOU HAVE HAD THE CHANCE TO LIVE THE EXTREME LIFE THESE LAST TWO DAYS, JAMMY DEVIL!...
WHILE WE OTHERS WERE LEFT BEHIND TO LIVE OUR DULL LIVES BEHIND OUR DESKS AND... HEY?
TCHAK
WHAT ARE...?
BETTY
TCHIK
NO! NOT THAT!... ARE YOU MAD!!!
I DIDN'T WANT TO BE THE ONLY PRIVILEGED ONE IN THE HOUSE!...
KLIK
YOUR TURN FOR A BIG ADVENTURE, MATHFOOL!...
TINK TIKTIKTIK TIK TAK TAK
W.E. MATHFOOL
46.
HELP!
NOT SO QUICK MATHFOOL, TAKE YOUR TIME!... AFTER ALL, YOU STILL HAVE...
...7 DAYS TO DIE!...
TCHIK TCHIK TAK
NO, NO, DON'T SHOOT! OPERATION MATHFOOL IS CANCELLED!...HAHAHA!
TURK
THE END
DE GROOT

PRINTED IN BELGIUM BY proost INTERNATIONAL BOOK PRODUCTION